PATSY
An American Tragedy

A musical
with related texts
on the deaths of JFK and others

by

Jack Lee

Edited by Eve Jackson
Additional lyrics by Stevie Stanley

Front cover design by John & Maggie Maizels

Published by:
Dead Fingers Press Limited
US Office: 340 Riverside Drive, NYC, NY 10025
Head Office: 54 Eade Road, London N4 1DH, UK

CONTENTS

ACKNOWLEDGEMENTS

There is no way Lee's wish to see his work published could have been achieved without the valiant support and practical common sense of Rosemary Chapman and Diana Finch, who spent many weekends plowing through mountains of paper, slaving at computers, giving technical support and offering creative and helpful suggestions. Xavier de la Huerga not only designed the Dead Fingers Press Logo and back cover but also provided much needed soup and tapas. Alan McPherson recovered essential data from ancient floppy disks and obsolete computers.

PREFACE

Jack (or Jackson) Lee was a teenager, already writing stories and dialogue, at the time of the deaths of Marilyn Monroe and President John F Kennedy. The mystery surrounding these events gripped his imagination, as did the later assassinations of Senator Robert Kennedy, Dr Martin Luther King and Malcolm X. In 1981 he began serious research into the deaths of the Kennedy brothers and the fate of others linked to them. At the time of his death he owned some 300 books on the principals of this drama, Jack and Bobby Kennedy, Marilyn, Lee Harvey Oswald, Jack Ruby, the Mafia, and the US secret services, along with articles and tape-recorded radio shows.

He made copious notes, and reworked the story in a variety of forms. In 1986 he drafted the outline of a screenplay entitled *Two Days in Dallas: History as Fiction*, or alternatively *Two Jacks and a Patsy*. In 1987-8 he wrote several versions of *A Little History*, a chronological account of the events surrounding the murder of JFK. The central, most dramatic section of *A Little History* was recorded on audiocassette, with Lee reading his text to a jazz backing played by Mike Hobart (tenor sax) and Martin Roser (alto sax) under the title "Jazz-So Stories." ("Jazz-So Stories" also included a satirical scene from Lee's novel *Baked Alaska*, and both pieces were performed at the North London Polytechnic in March 1987.) In 1988 came the outline of *Dallas: An American Tragedy*. All of these pieces are restricted to the events of the year 1963.

By 1986, however, Lee was already thinking of a work involving more characters and a wider timeframe. Under the title *Legends* he drafted a dialogue between Monroe (or rather Norma Jeane) and the Producer Joseph Schenck, along with extensive notes for a film, and also a scene, with an introduction of several paragraphs, entitled "The Recruiting Officer." This dialogue involves Oswald and a figure who could be David Ferrie, and was later to be reworked as a more succinct scene in *Patsy*. He also wrote a short piece on Jack Ruby, and explored a plotline according to which Ray Charles's song "Ruby" was used to trigger post-hypnotic suggestions in Oswald.

In the late eighties Lee considered writing a book on the general subject of *Assassins*, starting with the origins of the word in the deeds of the Hashashins of Alamut in Iran, and focusing particularly on the spate of assassinations in the United States in the 1960s. A literary agent sent his synopsis out to a number of publishers without success. All the while he was thinking of a dramatic presentation.

The idea of writing a musical had first come to Lee in his twenties, when he and his friend the musician and arranger Robert Kirby discussed writing one together, under the pseudonyms of Dan O'Man and Red McReady. Its title was *Godrocosmos* and it featured the planets. In 1991, now wanting to take further the dramatic presentation of his assassination material under the title *Patsy*, he proposed to a composer of his acquaintance the possibility of their working together to create a musical drama, with the intention that the composer would write the music and Lee would write the book and lyrics. The collaboration eventually foundered.

In 1997 Lee prepared the present version of his work for publication. After a decade of work pressures and deteriorating health, in September 2008 he was about to go ahead with the publication when death intervened. As the text was not yet 100% ready to print, minor changes have been necessary which it is hoped would be in accord with the author's wishes. The notes in the appendix were found at the end of the text and represent earlier ideas as to content which Lee might have incorporated, some of which exist as scenes in earlier versions of the play. Some lyrics have been omitted due to possible copyright difficulties. Those indisputably written by Lee alone have been retained, together with some new lyrics by Stevie Stanley.

Much of the dialogue is based closely on reports of events, but obviously the interpretation is Lee's own, the characters issuing from his own imagination. Central to the plot as he developed it are the parallel figures of Marilyn and Oswald, two dreamers caught up in a web of politics, crime and subterfuge they do not fully understand, and Jack Ruby, who dreams of becoming a big shot and is likewise duped. The scenes are in chronological order, the overarching motif of the Fates creating a unifying structure to a complex story in which the desires and activities of politicians, secret service agents and the mafia are interwoven.

Eve Jackson
April 2009

TWO JACKS AND A PATSY

Screenplay Outline

The events of Dallas, from noon on November 22nd 1963 to noon November 24th 1963, are presented according to the complete historical record of witnesses' and documentary accounts in a chronological sequence of scenes. Actions and words are accurate, according to earliest accounts, and faithfully depicted from each viewpoint. Main characters such as Oswald and Ruby are shown in these scenes, but not identified except as actually occurred. [Oswald played by Dustin Hoffman?]

The interrogation of Oswald and testimony of Ruby to Warren are also presented, providing the opportunity for flashbacks in which each respectively is shown to be involved in a web of intrigue and false appearance. Oswald has a history of military intelligence stretching back to his marine days in Japan when he learnt Russian and subscribed to Soviet journals with the tacit approval of the authorities (in California, the Monterey Institute) and was stationed at Atsugi, Japan, a U2 base, and may have spent unexplained periods of time at the Kamiseya base nearby, an NSA installation from which the Soviet radar defense system was monitored and its ground-stations located when aircraft deliberately entered their airspace. At this time he gained a relatively high security clearance, and may have been inducted into a language-monitoring role in SIGINT and sent for language training at Monterey. In New Orleans he is associated with David Ferrie, Maurice Bishop and George de Morenschildt, all of whom are spooks, and by association through 544 Camp Street with the anti-Castro Cubans (we see the set-up fight between them and him as he distributes FPCC leaflets with this address on, and with Ferrie he trains them at Lake Pontchartrain, and perhaps visits an arms dump in a house nearby) and with Guy Banister, who allows him to use office to prepare his FPCC literature (we see him and the Cubans in the corridors, the best of friends). At this time he becomes an FBI stooge through Banister. We see the connections between the spooks, the Cubans, the American right and the mob in the anti-Castro nexus, and we see Oswald's part of it. We see his "defection" to Russia and the letter promising to reveal secrets, his presence in Moscow when Gary Powers is captured from a downed U2, and his return to the US with Marina, his Russian wife, and daughter, with no official problems. We see him employed at Jaggars, Chiles, Stovall, dealing with U2 photos and assembling his collection of cameras, including a Minox, which the police find in his room. On the 22nd we see him engaged in some shady business leading up to his going to the Texas Theater to meet someone, there to be arrested. He has been in there for some time when someone else enters, running from the scene of the Tippit killing (where a man looking like Jack Ruby is seen), shortly before the police arrive.

After Oswald, the testimony of witnesses is taken by the police and FBI, and we see the establishment of a cover-story to blame Oswald; we know it is false because we have seen the events through the witnesses' eyes, and we also see the coercion or distorted reporting of the investigators, and the leakage of information to the press. We see also the letter from Katzenbach to Moyers in which the aims of the Commission are set out as to reassure the public that no conspiracy existed and to satisfy them that Oswald acted alone.

Ruby is shown, in flashback, as a gunrunner to Castro for the mob, then against him, visiting Trafficante in detention camp outside Havana with Lewis McWillie; meeting with Bernard Weissmann and J D Tippit at his club (to discuss the anti-Kennedy advert and the impeach Warren sign), as well as treating other cops; buying eavesdropping equipment and making lots of phone calls in the months prior to the assassinations. In real time we have seen him at the hospital, in the police station (bringing sandwiches for the cops; spelling Captain Fritz's name and correcting a police statement about Oswald's membership of the anti-Castro Free Cuba Committee for the press; trying to get in to the interrogation room; shooting Oswald) and making a phone call from a garage in which he says, about the time of Oswald's transfer, "I'll be there." The flashbacks occur especially when he pleads with Warren to take him back to

Washington (it is Warren's last day in Dallas) where he will feel safe to tell "the true facts."

The screenplay ends as Warren leaves for Washington as it began with Kennedy arriving from there. Headlines announce Commission findings.

There is some evidence that Oswald expected to be arrested in the Texas Theater. This is a standard way of bringing an undercover informer, without suspicion, for debriefing, and this may have been the purpose of the fracas in New Orleans between Oswald and Carlos Bringuier.

Also, through FBI sources, present the phone-bug conversation in which Trafficante threatens that Kennedy will be hit and that a nut will be set up to take the blame (perhaps flashback during testimony of FBI agent) and also show the Mexico City charade being constructed and issued by the CIA station there to Dallas police on the morning of the JFK hit (we see the cable come in).

During first sequence or intercut with it, show Ferrie's trip across the south and his arrest.

Jackson Lee
1 July 1986

A LITTLE HISTORY

October 3, 1963.

Lee Harvey Oswald arrives alone in Dallas from New Orleans, no money, no forwarding address.

October 4, 1963.

Sitting in the Carousel Club after putting paid to a bottle of liquor with Shirley Maudlin, his companion and a Dallas attorney, Carol Jarnagin overheard Jack Ruby in conversation at a table ten feet away. The other man, who gave the name H L Lee, said he had just arrived in Dallas from New Orleans. He wasn't dressed for nightclubbing, looked unkempt, needed a haircut, the attorney remembered thinking. He was broke; Jack offered him a job, cash on completion. Lee wanted half up front, now.

The job was to shoot the Governor from a rooftop, maybe The Carousel Club, as he rode through Dallas. Lee had his doubts, and anyway, why? Ruby said the Governor wouldn't do business with "the boys in Chicago" to "open up this State"; he wouldn't "work with us on paroles" to "get the right boys out" to do it. Business was bad for the boys, Chicago had the lid clamped on, Cuba was closed. "Look at this place, half empty…" The Governor was too straight, been in Washington too long, got to thinking like the Attorney General, "now there's a guy the boys would like to get." Wouldn't killing the Governor "put the heat on, too?" asks Lee. "Not really, they'll think some crackpot or communist did it, and it'll be written off as an unsolved crime." "That is, if I get away." "You'll get away."

The Attorney, who was proud of his memory, later recognized Lee Oswald from news photos, and wrote to the FBI on December 3rd. November 1963.

Sometime in November, Ruby and Oswald each rented a Post Box at the Dallas Terminal Annex. Was this the Post Office depot at the railway station? Did they go together? What were the numbers, and that of the Impeach Warren sign sponsors? See General Walker testimony.

One Tuesday or Thursday in the first two weeks in November, Wilbur Walden Litchfield sat down near Ruby's office at the Carousel Club, ready for a 10.00pm appointment to see him about a nightclub venture.

Three others were waiting, and went in before him; a friend of Ruby's from California, a magazine photographer who was taking pictures of the strippers, and a man who stood out from the rest, sloppily dressed in a white v-neck sweater, with uncombed hair. After fifteen or twenty minutes, Ruby and the man emerged and walked past Litchfield, two feet away, under a bright light. The man was "in his middle twenties, 5' 7" – 5' 9" and very slender," Litchfield stated in an affidavit on December 2nd, after he had recognized Lee Oswald from news photos on the TV and in the papers. The police gave him a polygraph test and concluded he had been "untruthful." They wouldn't accept his identification, repeating "Are you positive? Are you positive?" as he persisted "It looks like him." They threatened him "a Federal charge"; "you know, if you say you're positive and it wasn't him…"

November 15.

Bill DeMar's act at the Carousel Club features a routine where he remembers twenty objects named in rapid order by members of the audience. One of these patrons, who calls out a name, is Lee Oswald, whose face he recognizes on TV as Ruby shoots him.

November 16.

Dallas police officer, Billy R. Grammer is sitting with another cop in an all-night restaurant near the Police Department, about two in the morning. Jack Ruby comes in, introduces himself and pays for their meal.

November 19.

Ruby makes a phone call to Mrs. Billy Chester Carr, a booking agent in Houston.

November 21.

Early in the morning, Bruce Karlin in Houston telephoned the Carousel Club.

Around noon Jack Ruby left Dallas and drove to Houston. During the afternoon and early evening, he hung around Milam Street, on the four hundred block near the Rice Hotel, where the President was staying. At 2.30pm he made a phone call to the booking agents he had called two days before. A Houston Deputy saw him two or three times and talked with him at about 3pm. Others spoke to him also. He asked about a man called Jack who ran a club on Washington Street, said he had a Cadillac round the corner, showed money. One man saw a scar on the left of Ruby's face, faint amongst the stubble.

He asked Gloria Reece if she was going to a dinner at the Coliseum, where the President would be. She said she hadn't been invited, but maybe he'd like to buy her a beer, talk about a date. Ruby hurried off toward the Coliseum.

Later that night, after the President was safe in his hotel, ten Secret Service men relaxed and enjoyed themselves at the Cellar Door Club in Fort Worth, to which the owner had invited them. They drank a house special, "Salty Dicks," a grapefruit cocktail, on the house, which the owner swore was non-alcoholic. Five men from the next day's back-up car were among them. They left between 2.45 and 5am, to be on duty again by 8. The Cellar Door Club owner told a Carousel Club stripper that he expected to be questioned about getting them drunk on purpose.

November 22.

About 1.30am, a young man came into the Lucas B & B Restaurant, Dallas, and sat down alone. He was in his twenties, medium build, about 140 lbs., 5' 7" – 5' 9", with brown hair. Mrs. Mary Lawrence, the head waitress, noticed a small scar near his mouth as she asked him what he wanted. He said he was waiting for Jack Ruby, a regular customer she knew. An hour later Ruby appeared, looked at the young man, sat near the cash register and ordered an orange juice instead of his usual food; he didn't feel good. The man came over to join Ruby, and the cashier had a good look at him. The man ate; Ruby paid the bill. Mrs. Lawrence recognized the man as Lee Oswald from news photos after his arrest, and contacted the police and FBI.

After staying overnight in Fort Worth, the President rose and made a brief speech on the steps of his hotel, accompanied by the Governor of Texas and the Vice-President, also a favorite son of the state.

During the morning, the President's attention was drawn to a black-bordered newspaper advertisement headed "Welcome Mr President" and accusing him and his brother, the Attorney General, of being "soft on Communism." The President laughed and said, "We're really in nut country now!"

The Presidential party later took a short flight to Dallas, landing at Love Field shortly after eleven. It was a fine clear bright November day and crowds of people had gathered to see him and his wife.

Some way along his route, two men in a car drove into a parking lot by a railway overpass and backed up to a picket fence, got out to wait for the President to pass by.

People gradually congregated all along the route, which had been published in the local paper, but changed at the last minute so as to take a small detour off Main Street, along Houston and left along Elm to take it under the railway overpass.

This would take the motorcade onto a more direct route to the Trade Mart, its planned destination, and meant not having to make an illegal right turn.

Also it wouldn't take them under another bridge on which someone had hung a banner saying "Impeach the Chief Justice."

They didn't want to upset the President.

That morning, driving along Elm Street, a woman noticed a green truck by the curb and a man with a gun-case climbing up the small knoll, through the shrubbery and behind a wooden picket fence round a parking lot to one side of the overpass. She later recognized the men from news photographs; the man with the gun looked like Lee Oswald, the driver, Jack Ruby.

Later, on the knoll, a young soldier on leave tried to get into the parking lot to get a better view for his movie camera. He wanted to get some good shots on film to show his unit when he went back from leave. It was his hometown, and he wanted to show them how well they could treat a President down there.

He was stopped by a secret service man with dirty fingernails who said, "You can't go here. Stay the other side of the fence."

After placing a regular weekend ad for his clubs in the Morning News, Jack Ruby hung around the newspaper offices, chatting and passing angry comment on the black-bordered ad in the morning edition. A while after noon, sitting in a chair by a secretary's desk with a view towards the Book Depository four blocks away, Jack Ruby watched the parade.

Running parallel, a block apart through downtown Dallas, Elm, Main and Commerce Streets cross Houston Street, and emerge into the open space of Dealey Plaza, converging like the tines of a fork to pass under a broad railway bridge.

The President's car turned right from Main Street into Houston, passing the reflecting pools which flank Dealey Plaza, turning left in front of the Texas School Book depository. It came down towards the railway overpass and slowed almost to a halt as it passed the grassy knoll to the right.

People waved and cheered, took photographs and films, and the people in the motorcade waved back.

The Governor's wife turned in her seat and said to the President, "You can't say that Dallas doesn't love you." He replied, "That's obvious."

As his car passed by a road sign on the right, something caught the President's eye amongst the people on a flight of steps leading up the grassy knoll. He turned to glimpse a blonde woman in a polka dot dress, waving a red book. She could have been Marilyn. His hand froze in mid wave, and he began to turn away.

On the roof of the Book Depository, the Hertz sign shows the time at 12.30.

Just below the picket fence, in front of the parking lot, on the railway overpass, the solider on leave throws himself to the ground. He has trained under fire and had just felt the whiz as a bullet passed by from behind him. Then he heard the shot.

The President's hands go to his throat. He says, "I'm hit!" The Governor hears a shot, then feels himself hit.

There is a flurry of shots and the sky darkens as pigeons take off in a clatter. People take cover. Near the soldier, a pair of young parents lie over their son to protect him; a schoolteacher turns to her friend, saying, "Get down, they're shooting!" and then looks over the President, up at the knoll where she heard the shots come from.

At the moment of the first shot, a reporter takes a Polaroid picture of the President's car with the knoll in the background. When the shooting stopped, she ran across the road up the knoll where she had seen a man running.

In a tower overlooking the road and the overpass, a signalman hears shots, and sees smoke from the fence, then a man running off with what looked like a gun. Railway hands on the bridge see the smoke there too.

The President jerks back, one side of his face flies off, his wife says, "Oh God!", makes a grab, but he's gone.

A secret service man jumps on the back of the limousine, pushes her back in and down; a cop on a motorbike splattered with blood. The motorcade rushes off, under the overpass to get to the hospital, but it's too late.

Another policeman, directing traffic in front of the book depository, looks up when he hears shots and runs up the road to the knoll through the people who've thrown themselves down on the pavement, and those on the hill going up to the fence, where a woman tells him she's seen the shots come from.

At the top, after climbing the six-foot fence he saw a man trying to leave the parking lot, and approached him. The man showed a secret service badge, so the officer lets him go. Another officer also saw secret service men in the area behind the fence on the knoll.

Near the fence he could smell where a gun had been fired and saw muddy footprints on the back of a car, "as if," he said, "someone had stood to get higher, maybe to look over the fence."

Much later he wondered perhaps, while he stood there, whether someone lay curled up with a gun in the boot; and maybe they were driven out still hidden when the car left, like all of the others, after the search was called off.

At The Dallas Morning News, people gather around the TV as the story comes in from Dealey Plaza. Ruby looks shaken. He is pale, sitting with dazed eyes.

In a while, he gets up to phone his club, saying he might close it. He calls his sister, holding out the phone so she can be heard crying, "My God, what do they want?"

Around 1.30pm Ruby is at Parkland Hospital, in the corridor near the Trauma Room where surgeons were working over the President's body. A White House reporter, an old Dallas hand, feels a tug at his sleeve. Turning to see a familiar face he says "Hi, Jack." They shake hands. Ruby looks sad, asks about the President, wonders whether he should close his club for the weekend. The reporter says he thinks so and hurries off.

A few minutes later a priest administers the last rites, and a moist-eyed Doctor reads a brief notice of the President's death.

Lee Oswald sat in the stalls of the Texas cinema in Oak Cliff, watching a B movie, about half an hour after the President had been declared dead at Parkland Hospital. Shortly after that, a police patrol car driver had been shot dead as he got out of his car, having pulled up to speak with the man who shot him.

A truck driver who came on the scene knew how to work the patrol car radio, and alerted the police. Sometime later, a shoe store manager heard police sirens and saw a man looking flustered lingering by his display window, apparently hiding his face from the passing police. He followed the man, and saw him duck into the cinema without paying.

The shoe store manager told the cashier, who had left her booth to watch the police go by, and she phoned to tell them. When they arrived, the manager took them to the auditorium, the house lights went up and the shoe store manager went on the stage to point out the man he had seen.

Police officers fanned out and approached several people before one of them, gun in hand, came to Lee Oswald. Soon, six officers were over powering him, and as he was hustled out he shouted, "I am not resisting arrest!"

Several hours later, one of the police handed in a pistol he said Oswald had been waving around.

Jack Ruby spends the afternoon and evening at The Police Department. Reporters see him outside Captain Fritz's office on the third floor, where Oswald is being questioned. As he tries to open the door, someone says, "You can't go in there, Jack."

Later in the evening, on the third floor and in the elevator, cops say hello to Jack and chat with him.

Around midnight, the police brought Oswald out for a press conference. Ruby was there, wearing glasses and carrying his gun. When the DA said Lee had belonged to the Free Cuba Committee, Jack interrupted "That's Fair Play Cuba." After all, he knew it made a difference; they represented opposite sides.

After the conference, Ruby rushes up to the DA. "Hi, Henry." They shake hands. "Don't you know me? I'm Jack Ruby, I run the Vegas Club."

"What are you doing here?" Ruby's arm sweeps the room. "I know all these fellows."

He goes around handing out his club cards – invitations for free drinks, in pink with black lace borders and a picture of a stripper. He laughs and jokes.

November 23.

At the Police Department around 5 in the afternoon, a TV newsman sees Ruby go into the office where the DA is, a room off-limits to the press.   Later in the evening at the Police Department, the switchboard is flooded with calls offering information or threatening Oswald.   Extra staff are on duty.   One caller asked the woman switchboard operator to look around the room and tell him the name of officers there; he wanted to speak to someone he knew.   She put him through to Grammer, who recognized the voice, but couldn't place it. Who was the caller? "I can't tell you that, but you know me. We're going to kill Lee Harvey Oswald in the basement tomorrow." How? As the caller described the plans to transfer Oswald, about which Grammer didn't know, he got Lt Putnam to listen in. "First of all, there is a decoy, with lights and sirens and escorts, but Oswald ain't in it. He comes out later in an unmarked car."

Grabber asked again, "Who is this?"

"It makes no difference, but you're going to have to make some other plans, or we're going to kill Oswald right there in the basement. I hope there won't be a lot of shooting, but you can avoid that, because some officers could get hurt or killed, and they don't deserve that." He hung up.

Lt Putnam told Grammer the caller knew what he was talking about; Grammer typed up a report that they took to Chief Curry, surrounded by reporters in his office. The FBI and Sheriff's office had taken similar calls.   Grammer went home to bed, and was wakened by his wife, who had come home from church with their children and heard on the radio about Ruby shooting Oswald. As he watched the TV replays, Grammer remembered Ruby buying him a meal and realized whose voice he'd heard making threats on the phone.

November 24.

As the time approaches 11.30am, Lee Oswald is brought down in an elevator to the basement of the police building. An armored car is waiting on an exit ramp to act as decoy, but the unmarked car, which should be waiting for Oswald, is not in position outside the jail office through which he will come. The basement is packed with cops, press, TV crews and equipment, lights and cameras on the office door.

As the elevator touches down and Oswald steps out, Tom Howard, watching through the office window says, "That's all I wanted to see," turns and goes. Others push forward.

As Oswald steps from the office, a cop on each side behind him, hands cuffed in front of his v-neck, his left eye dark and puffy, a car horn sounds and another car squeals down one of the ramps. Oswald and the cops look to their right and Ruby comes out from behind a cop in the crowd to their left. He rushes forward, holding his gun at arm's length, a yard or so from Lee's chest, and fires once.

Lee and the cops turn to face Jack, looking stunned. Lee clutches his chest, his face a mask of pain, his knees buckling. He falls, blood between his fingers, and a cop bends over him. As Jack is wrestled to the ground by cops, he says "I'm Jack Ruby. You all know me."

As Bill DeMar watches TV at his Dallas motel, he recognizes Lee Oswald as a man in the audience at the Carousel Club, nine days before, who had called out an object for DeMar to remember. As he watches, Jack Ruby steps outs and shoots, Lee Oswald falls. Bill DeMar rushes into the motel office, tells the manager and then goes to his cabin to telephone an old friend, David Hoy, news director at Radio WIKY in Evansville, Indiana, at 11.32am.

In a welter of local and long-distance calls that fill the day, DeMar and Hoy are repeatedly in contact. Hoy gets the operator to cut in on one call, saying it's an emergency. Both call the Dallas Police Homicide Division twice, Hoy calls associated press in Indianapolis around noon, telling Dale Burgess what DeMar has told him. Hoy tells DeMar that he should hide out. He is in danger from underworld friends of Jack's, who might want him dead because of what he knew.

December 3, 1963.

Mrs Mary Lawrence, who is to be interviewed in 2 days time by the FBI about having seen Ruby and Oswald together at the Lucas B&B Restaurant early on November 22, receives a phone call. She hears a man tell her, "If you don't want to die, you'd better get outta town."

Jackson Lee
London, 31.1.87 (Revised 8.2.87; 1.3.87; 6.2.88)

DALLAS: AN AMERICAN TRAGEDY

Outline

During two days in Dallas, President John F Kennedy and Lee Harvey Oswald are caught in the crossfire of history. Time lines intersect in these moments, lives touch as people die. Can we trace these lives, in their everyday detail and through significant events, to this synchrony?

Jack Leon Ruby, born Jacob Rubinstein in Chicago, grew up tough, earning respect among street kids as a fighter, picking up cash from Al Capone for running errands. Soon he was running bets, later arms to Cuba, dope to the States and finally a pair of nightclubs in Dallas. In the basement of Police headquarters he ran into Lee Oswald, for the last but perhaps not for the first time. As officers dragged him to the floor he told them, "You know me, I'm Jack Ruby."

Lee Harvey Oswald, born in New Orleans, grew up there and later in New York City. His widowed mother remarried but for the most part brought up Lee, his brother and stepbrother, by herself. Lee, like the others, was at times fostered by relatives or in a home, and attended both public schools and military academy. At the age of 16, having read his older brother's Marine Corps manual, he persuades his mother to endorse his under-age application to sign up.

As a Marine, Lee is clearly not made of fighting stuff; he never manages to score more than the lowest grade with a rifle, and is remembered by his comrades for missing the target altogether. They recall him also as quiet and studious, not much of a mixer. He was sent to a secret language school in California, spoke Russian and subscribed to a variety of Soviet and US communist publications, which he received by mail at his barracks. He was known as "Oswaldkovich."

Oswald's unit served at the Atsugi airbase, Japan, from which U2 spy aircraft took off for reconnaissance flights over Russia, to take photographs and test the Soviet radar defenses. Oswald was a radio operator with security clearance at "crypto" level, higher than others in his unit. Atsugi was also used by the CIA for tests of possible truth drugs, including LSD, as part of their mind-control project "Artichoke." During this period Lee had an active social life off base and a Japanese girlfriend. He also spent some time in the guardhouse for wounding himself with his own gun and for pouring a drink over a sergeant. Shortly after his discharge, Lee Oswald appeared in Moscow announcing that he wished to defect, telling the US embassy that he was prepared to reveal the secrets he had learned as a Marine. Although the diplomats treat him lightly, military codes are changed around the world.

After slashing his wrists in his hotel bathroom Lee is allowed to stay in Russia, working in a radio factory in Minsk and marrying a Russian pharmacist, Marina, with whom he had a daughter, before deciding to return to the US. They did so without hindrance, landing in New York and travelling south.

In New Orleans Lee has a job at the Riley Coffee Company and hangs about next door at a garage where the Secret Service keep their cars, reading gun magazines. None of his jobs lasts long. At Riley he just oils machines, but at Jaggars-Chiles-Stovall, a photographic and printing company, he uses skills apparently acquired in the service and has access to a classified section of the works where names from government lists are set onto aerial photographs of Cuba.

Lee keeps a notebook, in which the word "microdot" appears next to "Jaggars-Chiles-Stovall." There are also addresses relating to a variety of anti-Castro organizations. Lee wrote to the New York headquarters of the "Fair Play for Cuba Committee," asking for official support in his attempts to organize a New Orleans chapter; despite refusal he has leaflets printed and distributes them. During one such street demonstration he is confronted by an angry anti-Castro activist, Carlos Bringuier. Oswald takes it calmly, saying, "If you want to hit me, Carlos, it's okay." He is arrested, and demands to see the FBI, who send an agent to interview him in jail. Among the items Oswald gives the agent is one of his leaflets with the address 544 Camp Street. The building at this site houses a number of offices, including those of the CIA, and of Guy Banister, a private detective, former FBI agent and right-wing activist. Oswald and Bringuier had been seen in these corridors together.

During this time also, the spring and summer of 1963, Oswald or someone resembling him attended and spoke at anti-Castro student meetings, was seen at an anti-Castro guerrilla training camp and renewed an association with David Ferrie. Ferrie was a pilot, and had been the commander of a Civil Air Patrol cadet corps to which Oswald had belonged briefly as a youth in New Orleans. Ferrie had lost all his hair, which he replaced with a fuzzy red wig, and his eyebrows, which he painted on with mascara. He had been sacked from his airline job and repeatedly arrested for homosexuality; the city directory listed Ferrie as a psychologist, he claimed to be a hypnotist and to have a Ph.D., and now worked as a private detective for Carlos Marcello, Mafia boss of Louisiana and former operator of casinos in Cuba. At this time someone resembling Oswald was seen by a hip New Orleans lawyer, hanging out with a group of young gay Latin men.

In the autumn of 1963 someone giving Oswald's name travels to Mexico and tries unsuccessfully to get a visa for Cuba and Russia. This man is photographed by a CIA watching post as he leaves the Cuban consulate; it is not Lee Oswald. Lee goes to Dallas, mixes with the White Russian exile community and is befriended by George de Morenschildt, a former espionage agent and now geologist, much travelled in Latin America. Marina Oswald is taken up by Ruth Paine, a Quaker active in the Russian-American friendship movement, who finds Lee a job at the Texas School Book Depository. After his arrest, asked by journalists whether he had shot the President as he passed by the Depository, Lee said, "I haven't killed anyone. I'm just a patsy."

In the few months while he was in Dallas, Lee had again been impersonated by someone who drew attention to himself and sometimes gave, or was called by, the name Oswald. This man, who was often reported as being untidy and unshaven, while Lee was always neat and clean, drove a car at reckless speed during a test drive and made remarks about being back in Russia, fired expertly at other people's targets on a shooting range, inquired about fitting a rifle with a telescopic sight, threw up in a Cuban exile bar and was introduced to the daughter of a jailed opponent of Castro as a crazy man who thought Kennedy should be killed for creating the Bay of Pigs disaster. This lady identified a photo of Oswald as the man called "Leon" only after investigators drew in stubble and messy hair. According to the FBI, Lee Harvey Oswald was not in Dallas at the time of this meeting, nor could he have been present at other sightings.

John Kennedy was elected President in 1960 by a narrow margin over Richard Nixon, the votes of Cook County, Illinois, which included Chicago, being crucial to his victory. According to many, his father, former ambassador Joseph P Kennedy, had bought these votes from the mob, via Chicago Mayor Richard Daley and Mafia boss Sam Giancano. On his inauguration the CIA presented him with a plan for the invasion of Cuba and overthrow, perhaps assassination, of Fidel Castro. He appointed his brother Robert Attorney-General, and a war against organized crime began, its main targets being Carlos Marcello and Jimmy Hoffa, leader of the Teamsters' Union. Marcello was briefly kidnapped by Justice Department agents and flown to Guatemala; Ferrie flew him back. Both Marcello and Hoffa made threats against the Kennedys. At the same time, Sam Giancana, another Mafioso John Rosselli and former FBI agent Robert Maheu were employed by the CIA with the Kennedys' knowledge in a plot to assassinate Castro. After Kennedy failed to provide promised air cover for the CIA-planned exile invasion at the Bay of Pigs, and later backed down in the Cuban missile crisis, both the exile Cubans and their CIA backers were angry with the President; the mob also felt double-crossed not to have got back their Cuban casinos, brothels and drug routes, and felt foolish having been strung along on a contract which came to nothing for the men who were dragging them through the courts.

These were not the only people betrayed by the Kennedy brothers. Both had promised to marry Marilyn Monroe, although they were already married; both promised to divorce, despite being Catholic. Marilyn had met John first of all, through Frank Sinatra, a mutual friend who acted, according to the President's brother-in-law actor Peter Lawford, as Kennedy's pimp. Later she was passed on, in the family tradition, to Bobby. Marilyn became pregnant and had an abortion in Mexico. She talked to her psychiatrist about very important people who had come into her life, but seemed about to ruin it; she played him tapes which may have come from a bug she had installed in her home. Other tapes, confiscated by Federal agents from Bernard Spindel, wireman to the mob, and Jimmy Hoffa, preserve the moments of Marilyn's death.

In the evening before her death in 1962, Marilyn is visited by Bobby Kennedy and another man, perhaps a doctor. She does not want to see him. She is through with him and his brother. She will call a press conference to tell the world how they have let her down. Bobby is hysterical, his voice a squeal. There are sounds of a scuffle, someone being struck and falling. Bobby says, "What are we going to do with the body?" After making a phone call he leaves and is later helicoptered out from the beach near Peter Lawford's house. Lawford claims that Marilyn had earlier told him over the phone that she had taken the last of her sleeping pills and asked him to "say goodbye to the President."

An ambulance is called and takes Marilyn off, she may still be alive, but dies en route. She is brought back and arranged on the bed. The phone is placed in her right hand, which she never used for this purpose in life. A private investigator removes from her house any compromising items, including her big red diary. A locksmith changes locks on drawers, filing cabinets, closets. Finally her housekeeper calls her doctors, who declare her dead and call the authorities. The autopsy shows no traces of sleeping pills in the gut, but the blood carries a heavy dose of barbiturate. In her last completed film, The Misfits, she wears a polka-dot dress.

Six years later Bobby is back in Los Angeles for the California primary elections, in which he is standing for the presidential nominee. He takes some time out to travel alone to a small town, apparently to check out a story about his brother's death. After making his victory speech, Bobby is taken through the kitchens of the Ambassador Hotel, where a girl in a polka-dot dress stands on a tray-stacker next to Sirhan Sirhan as he starts to shoot. Bobby is pulled down by his bodyguard, who at the same time shoots him in the head from behind. Bobby turns as he falls, grabbing the guard's clip-on necktie, which lies next to him as he lies dying in the TV lights. The girl in the polka-dot dress runs off, shouting, "We did it! We killed him!" She is not seen again.

Jack Lee
1988

PATSY
An American Tragedy

Musical

DRAMATIS PERSONAE

THE FATES: CLOTHO
                  LACHESIS
                  ATROPOS

NORMA JEANE/MARILYN MONROE (film star)

JACOB RUBENSTEIN/JACK RUBY (nightclub owner, Mafia link)

LEE HARVEY OSWALD (framed as assassin of Jack Kennedy)

FRUITSELLER

JACK RUBY AGED 13

AL CAPONE (Chicago Mafia boss)

RUBY'S PAL 1

RUBY'S PAL 2

JIM DOUGHERTY (Norma Jeane's Husband)

PSYCHOLOGIST

LEE OSWALD AS AN ADOLESCENT

SAM GIANCANA (Chicago Mafia boss)

DAVID FERRIE (pilot and secret agent)

PETER LAWFORD (film actor)

JACK KENNEDY (President of the USA)

SENATE COMMITTEE CHAIRMAN

BOBBY KENNEDY (Senator and brother of Jack Kennedy)

CARLOS MARCELLO (Mafia boss in New Orleans)

TWO ATTORNEYS

JUDY CAMPBELL (girlfriend of Giancana)

MARINA OSWALD (Russian wife of Lee Oswald)

US CONSULAR OFFICER

SANTO TRAFFICANTE (Mafioso linked to plots against Castro)

DOCTOR

ADVERTISING CLERK

JUDGE

NEWSREADER (VOICE)

LEON, LEE's double

HENRY WADE (District Attorney)

REPORTER

EARL WARREN (head of enquiry in deal of JFK)

GERALD FORD (congressman and future president)

COPS
LAWYER
DOCTOR
NURSE
SIRHAN SIRHAN (convicted of assassination of Bobby Kennedy)
GUARD
GIRL IN POLKA DOT DRESS

RUNNING ORDER

SONGS	CHARACTERS

ACT ONE

Prelude

	Prologue	The Fates
	Looking for love	Marilyn Monroe
	Somebody	Jack Ruby
	Masquerade	Lee Oswald
	All assembled here	

Scene 1	Chicago Street Corner, 1924	
		Jacob (Age 13)
		Fruitseller
		Pal 1
		Pal 2
		Al Capone

Scene 2	Hollywood, 1944	
	Dreamer*	Norma Jeane
		Jim Dougherty

Scene 3	Chicago, 1946	
	A Jew can be a hero	Jack Ruby
		Sam Giancana

Scene 4	New York, 1952	
		Lee Oswald
		Psychologist

Scene 5	New Orleans, 1955	
		David Ferrie
	A secret life*	Lee Oswald

	SONGS	CHARACTERS
Scene 6	Malibu, 1955	Peter Lawford Marilyn Monroe Jack Kennedy The Fates

Scene 7	Washington, 1959	Congressional
		   Committee
		   Chairman
		Jack Kennedy
		Bobby Kennedy
		Jack Ruby
		Sam Giancana

	Tomato salesman	Carlos Marcello 2 Attorneys
Scene 8	Los Angeles, 1959	Jack Kennedy Judy Campbell Marilyn Monroe
Scene 9	Moscow, 1959 Masquerade	Lee Oswald The Fates US Consular Officer
Scene 10	Hollywood, 1960 Looking for love	Marilyn Monroe

Scene 11	Dallas/Havana, 1960
	   Somebody
	   The sweet life*
		Jack Ruby
		
		Santo Trafficante

	SONGS	CHARACTERS

Scene 12   Hollywood, August 4 1962

Marilyn Monroe
Bobby Kennedy
Doctor

ACT TWO

Scene 1   Dallas, Summer 1963
                     Three sisters

The Fates
Lee Oswald
Marina Oswald

Scene 2   New Orleans, Summer 1963

Sam Giancana
Santo Trafficante
Carlos Marcello
David Ferrie

Scene 3   New Orleans, Summer 1963

Lee Oswald
David Ferrie
Carlos Marcello

Scene 4   Los Angeles, Autumn, 1963
                     Watch out!*

Judy Campbell
Jack Kennedy

Scene 5   Dallas, November, 1963

The Fates
David Ferrie
Lee Oswald
Jack Ruby
Leon

	SONGS	CHARACTERS

Scene 6   Dallas, November 22, 1963
                    The moment I've   Lee Oswald
                       been waiting for*

                                           Marina Oswald

Scene 7   November 22, 1963

                                           Jack Ruby
                                           Clerk
                                           Judge
                                           Carlos Marcello
                                           David Ferrie
                                           Bobby Kennedy
                                           Newsreader
                                           Leon
            What's going on?*   Lee Oswald
                                           Cops
                                           Reporter
                                           Henry Wade

Scene 8   Dallas County Jail, Summer 1964
                    They don't wanna   Jack Ruby
                       know*

                                           Lawyer
                                           Chief Justice Warren
                                           Congressman Ford

Scene 9   Ruby's dream, 1966-67

                                           Jack Ruby
                                           Doctor
                                           Nurse
                                           David Ferrie
                                           Lee Oswald

	SONGS	CHARACTERS

Scene 10   Los Angeles, June 1968

	Three sisters	The Fates
		Carlos Marcello
		Sam Giancana
		Judy Campbell
		Bobby Kennedy
		Sirhan Sirhan
		Girl in polka dot dress
		Guard
		Reporter

Lyrics contributed by Stevie Stanley are marked with an *.

ACT ONE

ACT ONE, PRELUDE

DARKNESS. THE THREE FATES sit above the Hollywood sign, spinning, cutting and winding threads. They sing the PROLOGUE.

CLOTHO: From the tangled fleece of life I, Clotho, spin
Each thread, to clothe the soul in mortal flesh.
With me, each destiny begins.

LACHESIS: I, Lachesis, measure each thread to its
Full extent, and speak its destined lot.
Here, in my verdict, justice lives.

ATROPOS: To all whom birth has blessed comes death, when
Each allotted span is due. There is no appeal.
Then I, Atropos, cut the thread.

FATES: What is born to live, must die,
But how is not for us to say, nor why.

Enter MARILYN, opposite FATES. She pauses, turns to the audience and sings LOOKING FOR LOVE

MARILYN: So loved and yet so lonely,
So longed-for, but alone.
A million hearts desire me
But none beats with my own.

Looking for love
I'm yearning for love
I may never find love
But will love
Ever find me?

MARILYN turns to look at FATES
DARK
MARILYN walks to tableau

Enter JACK RUBY, turns to the audience and sings SOMEBODY

JACK RUBY: Somebody,
              Somebody to look up to.
              Somebody big,
              Somebody to respect.

              Somebody,
              Somebody with some chutzpah!
              Somebody fine,
              Somebody of the best...

JACK RUBY turns to look at FATES
DARK
JACK RUBY walks to Tableau

Enter LEE, turns to the audience and sings MASQUERADE:

LEE: All my own is the future,
              Mine to weave as a fable,
              Mine to hold as a mirror,
              Of the world as it's made.

              I can answer when life calls,
              Play my part for my country,
              I can live my own legend,
              In the great masquerade.

LEE turns to look at FATES
DARK
Lee walks to Tableau

At rear of stage, NORMA JEANE tableau is lit - a tall girl in a grey shift sits at a white upright piano, gazing at three framed photos on the lid - Abraham Lincoln, Clark Gable and Daddy. MARILYN is spot lit, turns to face the tableau.

THE FATES sing ALL ASSEMBLED HERE

LACHESIS: Look now on California,
                 The town of Hollywood,
                 Where Norma Jeane,
                 A lonely child,
                 Dreams of the great and good.

At rear, JACOB tableau is lit - a well-built young man, in a suit and hat, is keeping watch, nervously, outside an office door labeled 'Scrap Metal and Junk Handler's Union - Treasurer'; an arm pointing a gun at a man's head is silhouetted on the pane. JACK RUBY is spot lit, turns to face the tableau.

ATROPOS: See the sad brutal world
                 Of this unwanted son.
                 In Chicago Jacob lives
                 By the law of the gun.

At rear, LEE tableau is lit - a mother in a hospital bed, nursing a baby. LEE is spot lit, turns to tableau.

CLOTHO: A thread spun out in New Orleans,
                 Caught upon a thorn -
                 Lee Oswald's life
                 Is fragile, and
                 His destiny is torn.

FATES: All these threads will come together;
                 All the lives which now appear,
                 Will, by subtle winds of fortune

MARILYN, JACK RUBY and LEE turn to the front

FATES: And the chosen course they steer,
                 Be woven in a tragic pattern,
                 All are now assembled here.

ACT ONE, SCENE ONE
CHICAGO STREET CORNER, 1924

Day breaks. Sounds of late night revelers departing. A FRUITSELLER enters and sets up his stall. Enter JACOB, aged 13, PAL 1 and PAL 2. Music: Jazz Age Instrumental. Enter AL CAPONE, a tall, stout man with a deep scar on one cheek, wearing a long yellow vicuna coat and a white fedora. He stops across the street at the fruit stand, the FRUITSELLER hands him a bag of fruit, he looks inside it, nods and smiles.

JACOB: Who's that?

PAL 1: That's the biggest man in Chicago. He runs this town.

JACOB: Don't the Mayor run Chicago?

PAL 2: And what's the mayor's name if he's so big?

JACOB: His Honor Mister…

PAL 1: He ain't got no honor compared to Mister Al Capone…

PAL 2: Al Capone, he's a man of honor, a man of respect, if you're down he'll take care of you…

PAL 1: … if you're smart he'll be good to you, he's a hero.

JACOB: A hero! A real live hero?

PAL 1: A real Italian hero.

PAL 2: And you can bet he don't like kikes.

JACOB turns and flashes a flurry of blows on PAL 2, who falls to the ground. JACOB stands over him. CAPONE approaches. PAL 1 exits, running.

JACOB: Don't you use those bad words…

CAPONE: Hello boys. You makin' trouble on my streets?
              You're the sparky one, what's your name?

He holds out the bag of fruit. Jacob loads his pockets.

JACOB: Jacob, sir. Jacob Rubenstein. I had to hit him sir, he
              insulted me, my family, my people. He said…

CAPONE: It don't matter what he said, he'll know better now. I
              like you. I feel like that too. It's the most important
              thing, to stand up for yourself, your family, your
              people, the most important thing. You may not come
              from the best family, but it's your family. Your
              people, they may not be the most swell people, but
              they're your people. You got to stand up for who you
              are, defend your honor, your pride, that way you earn
              respect. Know who I am?

JACOB: Yes, sir, Mister Capone. They say you're a hero.

CAPONE: Do they? Like to earn a dollar, now and then?

JACOB: Sir?

CAPONE: You're a smart kid, and you can take care of yourself.
              I got errands for kids like you. See this package?

JACOB: Yes, sir.

CAPONE: Take it down to O'Banion's garage, know where that
              is?

JACOB: North Clark Street, sir.

CAPONE: Good. Give it to Hymie Weiss, and if you can't give
           it to him, don't give it to no one. Understand?

JACOB: Yes, sir. And if I can't give it to him…

CAPONE: Bring it back and give it to Giuseppe on the fruit
           stand, there. And if you do it right, he'll let you pick a
           bag of fruit – pick all the same sort and I'll know you
           did well. If you have trouble, mix the fruit. It's a
           dollar for you next time I'm by here. What do you
           say, Sparky? You wanna be a hero too?

JACOB nods, CAPONE tosses the packet and exits. PAL 2 gets up, dusts himself off, looks respectfully at JACOB and exits. JACOB hums A Jew can be a Hero theme and exits.

ACT ONE, SCENE TWO
HOLLYWOOD, 1944

NORMA JEANE and JIM sit in the bay window of their California apartment, looking out at the Pacific under a starry sky. He strums a guitar; she flips through screen magazines, gazing at photos of Clark Gable.

NORMA J: Isn't he handsome? A real star. You know, when I was a little girl, I used to think he was my Daddy? They had the same eyes, I thought, and that special smile, you know, as if it's meant just for you?

JIM stops strumming, picks up official-looking letter

JIM: Don't you know there's a war on? October 12, 1944, that's the date on these orders to sail. Tomorrow I'll be leaving for the Pacific, and all you can think about is tinsel town. Some marriage this is. Whenever I come back on leave you're always away yourself, on some beach, modeling swimsuits for some photographer, or hanging around the movie studios - they must be sick of you hustling them for an audition. It isn't right, Norma Jeane.

NORMA J: Oh Jim, it isn't that I don't love you, I do, and I love the work at the parachute factory too, doing what I can for all those other men like you, all doing what you can for our country, but even with the allowance you send me, it isn't enough.

JIM: Other men's wives don't seem to think so. It's just not enough for you, you always want something more.

NORMA J: I always have, Jim. I've always known that if I really try, if I really believe in myself and work hard, I could become a great actress, maybe not a star, but...

JIM: That's just a dream.

NORMA J: To you, maybe, but to me it's all there is. There are hundreds, thousands of women right here in California dreaming that same dream, some only for a moment, some for weeks, months, years, but I've been dreaming it all my life, and I'll make it come true, you know I will, because I'm dreaming the hardest.

They sing DREAMER

NORMA J: I've always been a dreamer
                  With stars on my mind.
                  When pictures from a dream
                  Flicker on the screen
                  I leave the dreary world behind.

JIM: You've always been a dreamer.
                  No matter what I do
                  Working day and night
                  To make your world feel right,
                  It's never been enough for you.

NORMA J: I'm dreaming of the movies,
                  Of shimmering on the screen,
                  Of dancing with the stars,
                  Of silk and champagne bars –
                  So everyone knows Norma Jeane.

ACT ONE, SCENE THREE
CHICAGO, 1946

An office. JACK RUBY stands in front of a desk, behind which sits SAM.

SAM: Hello, Jack, how's things?

JACK RUBY: Can't complain, boss.

SAM: Fine. Listen, Jack, the war's over, people want a good
                time. Fancy joints, broads, good booze, not like that
                rotgut we used to run in together from Cuba, eh....?

JACK RUBY kind of chuckles

SAM: ...and gambling. You've been a gambler all your life,
                Jack. The Organization wants you to front a new
                operation.

JACK RUBY: Yeah, but gambling's got no class, boss...

SAM: Maybe before, in the old days, but now.... You know
                Carlos got Texas and Louisiana sewed up, and Santo
                runs all the action in Havana. Carlos and me got
                plans for you, down south.

JACK RUBY: In New Orleans?

SAM: Dallas, Jack.

JACK RUBY: Oh man, they'll kill me.

SAM: We're depending on you, Jack. You'll be the big man
                in town. Fancy restaurant, casino, roulette, no more
                cheap slot machines.

JACK RUBY: Do you know what they do to Jews down there?
They think we have horns and tails.

SAM: But, hey, Jack, you're tough, and smart. You could
show them what a Jew could do in a hick town. It's
all set up for you, we got the sheriff squared.

JACK RUBY: The sheriff? What is this you're doing to me? Why?

SAM: Adios Jack. Be a hero. It's up to you.

JACK RUBY leaves the room, closes the door, shoots his cuffs, runs a hand over his hair, and sings A JEW CAN BE A HERO.

JACK RUBY: Cast among the lions, like Daniel of old,
Never wanting courage, his faith had made him bold.
Could I be a hero?
My chances could be zero
Or my name be wrought in gold

Oh to be a hero, like great Jonathan or Saul,
Oh to feel admiring eyes, to walk six cubits tall!
I could be a hero
Like David, without fear, oh
Making mighty giants fall!

Yes you can be a hero,
A Jew can be a hero,
A real Jewish hero too.

ACT ONE, SCENE FOUR
NEW YORK, 1952

LEE and a PSYCHOLOGIST sit at a low table, he rather stiffly in a modern-style wing chair, she on a matching settee. LEE is a tall and awkward thirteen; she is attentive. He has a polite southern accent, she a professional clipped New England. On the table are wooden blocks and rods in various colors, shapes and sizes, animal toys, dolls, books and magazines, a large sketchpad, paints, brushes, and crayons.

PSYCH: Well, Lee, make yourself comfortable… and I'm going to ask you some questions. Is that okay?

LEE: Yes, ma'am.

PSYCH: Lee, your school principal tells me you've been staying away, and he's worried about you. Now these tests we've just done show that you're a bright child, but you just have difficulty spelling. Is that why you miss school, Lee?

LEE: No, ma'am. I try and spell right, but somehow it never looks the way it should. I like school, but the other kids make fun of me.

PSYCH: What do they do, Lee?

LEE: Oh they make these horrible noises and say that's the way I speak, like hogs and chickens, and they say I dress like a country boy. They rag me. Some of them say I walk like a girl. I like to go to the zoo.

The PSYCHOLOGIST picks up a magazine with a picture on the cover of Norma Jeane wearing a sack stenciled "Miss Idaho Potato."

PSYCH: What do you feel when you look at this picture, Lee?

LEE: Sad.

PSYCH: Why's that, Lee?

LEE: Because she's outdoors, in the sun, feeling the breeze, and I'm not. I'd like to be.

PSYCH: Is there anything else you feel about her?

LEE: She has a nice smile, and pretty eyes.

They put down the magazine and the PSYCHOLOGIST looks at her notes, then at LEE directly.

PSYCH: Have you ever seen the television, Lee? Do you have a favorite program? One you really enjoy watching?

LEE: I do ma'am. "I Lived Three Lives."

PSYCH: And what do you enjoy about it? What makes it special for you, Lee?

LEE: Well, ma'am, it's about a secret agent, for the FBI, and each time you see him he's somebody else – it's exciting – always fighting, in a quiet way, for his country. Our country, ma'am.

PSYCH: Would you like to be…

LEE: Yes, ma'am!

PSYCH: … like him? Are you often alone, Lee? What do you do?

LEE: I like to take the subway. I look out the windows and wonder about things.

PSYCH: Do you sometimes go off into a dream, while you're
            sitting alone, where fantastic things happen?

LEE: Ma'am? I can take care of myself. I always know
            where I'm going, and to get back in time.

PSYCH: In time for what, Lee?

LEE begins to play with the toys on the table, flip through the magazines. The PSYCHOLOGIST looks at her watch and closes her notebook.

ACT ONE, SCENE FIVE
NEW ORLEANS, 1955

Interior, Civil Air Patrol hut.

FERRIE: *[off]* Air Cadet Company, attenn-shun. *[sound of boots stamping]* Dismiss. *[sound of boots walking off]* Cadet Oswald, step into my office.

Enter FERRIE and LEE

FERRIE: Lee Oswald, you're a good cadet.

LEE: Thank you, sir.

FERRIE: Honest, hardworking, and patriotic.

LEE: Thank you, sir.

FERRIE: You're a credit to your country, Cadet Oswald. *[pause]* Do you love your country, Lee?

LEE: Yes, sir, you know I do.

FERRIE: Lee, you're sixteen years old, time to think about life. Would you like to serve your country, Lee?

LEE: In any way I can, Captain Ferrie. I want to follow my brother Robert into the Marines, sir. I've read his Marine Corps Manual, sir, and I've learned a lot already. I wish I could join now, but they say I'm too young.

FERRIE: Ever thought of something more exciting, Lee?

LEE: I could be a flyer in the Marines, sir.

FERRIE: Ever thought of working undercover, Lee, for your country?

LEE: Kind of a secret agent, sir? A spy?

FERRIE: Much more than spying, Lee, and you've got what it takes, what I like in a boy. Can you keep a secret, Lee?

LEE: Yes, sir, Captain Ferrie.

FERRIE: You can be a flyer and a secret agent, Lee, like I was.

LEE: You, sir?

FERRIE: I was chosen, Lee, to be the test pilot for a secret plane that flies very high, higher than any radar or rocket or any other plane can go. That's how I lost my hair, Lee - did you know this was a wig?

LEE: Uhh...

FERRIE: I don't regret it - I did it for my country.

They sing A LIFE OF SECRETS

FERRIE: It's your chance to serve your country
In a special kind of way.

LEE: I could do something that matters
If it's really like you say.

FERRIE: You'll get lots of special training
Like not many people do.

LEE: I'd be proud to play my part, sir
Be an agent, just like you.

FERRIE: There'll be thrills and tough assignments,
           You'll be on a secret mission.

LEE: I'm prepared to meet such hardships -
           It's my secret ambition.

FERRIE: You'll have to be hard,
           Not ruled by your heart.

LEE: I'll be loyal and true,
           I'm ready to start.

FERRIE: You must learn to keep silent
           Give nothing away.

LEE: I'm at your command, sir,
           Whatever you say.

BOTH: No-one must know
           Where we go
           Who we are
           What we do -
           A secret life,
           A life for the few.

EXEUNT, FERRIE with arm on LEE's shoulder.

ACT ONE, SCENE SIX
MALIBU, 1955

A beach house. LAWFORD hosts a party, at which are MARILYN and JACK KENNEDY, standing together. THE FATES are amongst the guests. MUSIC: COCKTAIL PARTY - continues to end of scene.

MARILYN: Doesn't your lovely wife ever come with you on these campaign tours, Senator Kennedy?

JACK K: She prefers the east coast, the family, her horses...

LAWFORD approaches

LAWFORD: I see there's no need to introduce you...

JACK K: Frank Sinatra beat you to it, Peter.

LAWFORD shrugs, EXIT

JACK K: You must be the brightest star in Hollywood, just now, Marilyn.

MARILYN: Don't let's talk about that, the movies are a fantasy. Tell me, what's happening in Washington?

JACK K: Well, the most important thing is organized crime. My brother Bobby's going after them - the Mafia - in Congress. You know, they complain we're violating their civil rights? *[laughs]*

MARILYN: Civil rights are important, maybe not for the mob, but for Negros. It's almost a century after emancipation, and people are still treated differently because of their color, and they just want the same chance as everyone else.

JACK K: And I'm one of the few in Congress who try and make sure they do have that chance, but in a Republican administration...

MARILYN: Oh, you can't blame one party, Senator. They all support segregation - Lincoln was a Republican, remember. And he would have been called a Communist, now.

JACK K: Do you really think so?

MARILYN: Well, he was for the people, and the Communists, they're for the people too, aren't they?

JACK K: I must admit I've never heard Honest Abe called a Communist before, but what you say, and you say it so charmingly...

LAWFORD: *[off]* Oh Jack, Marilyn, you must meet Rita!

EXEUNT JACK KENNEDY and MARILYN, arm in arm.

ACT ONE, SCENE SEVEN
WASHINGTON, 1959

A high ceilinged, marble-walled Senate hearing room. The Congressional Committee on Organized Crime meets. Seated behind a long, raised, desk, are the CHAIRMAN, JACK KENNEDY and BOBBY KENNEDY. From time to time, JACK KENNEDY whispers and nods with the others.

Seated before the Committee are SAM, CARLOS, and their ATTORNEYS. Behind them, in the audience, sits JACK RUBY.

CHAIRMAN: *[raps gavel on desk]* The Congressional Committee on organized Crime is now in session. Honorable Robert F. Kennedy, Committee Counsel, will lead the questioning.

BOBBY: Mister Giancana, where were you born?

SAM: I decline to answer.

CHAIRMAN: You are ordered to answer. I want to tell you something now; we are not going to put up with this foolishness.

SAM: I decline to answer because I honestly believe my answer might tend to incriminate me. *[giggles]*

CHAIRMAN: You say it that way if you mean it that way.... Proceed.

BOBBY: Is there something funny about it, Mr Giancana?

SAM: I decline to answer on the grounds that it might tend to incriminate me.

BOBBY: Would you tell us if you have opposition from somebody you dispose of them by having them stuffed in a trunk? Is that what you do, Mister Giancana?

SAM: I decline to answer because I honestly believe my answer might tend to incriminate me. *[giggles]*

BOBBY: Would you tell us about any of these operations, or will you just giggle every time I ask you a question? I thought only little girls giggled, Mr Giancana.

SAM: I decline to answer because I believe...

BOBBY fumes, turns to CARLOS, who glares back, then smiles.

BOBBY: Mister Marcello, are you a member of the Mafia?

CARLOS: I refuse to answer the question on the ground it might incriminate me.

BOBBY: Mr Marcello, have you been able to use law enforcement officials to assist you in your business? Did the Jefferson Parish deputy sheriffs assist you in getting locations for your coin machines?

CARLOS: I refuse to.....

BOBBY: Do you realize that you are claiming a privilege under the Constitution of the United States, and you still have not ever sought to assume the responsibilities of citizenship. Isn't that correct?

CARLOS: I decline to answer the question.

BOBBY: According to information you have provided to State and Federal authorities, you reside or operate at a number of addresses in Louisiana. Where exactly do you live, Mr Marcello?

CARLOS: I refuse to answer the question on the ground that it may intend to criminate me. *[sic]*

SAM: *[giggles]*

BOBBY: According to our information, five years, nine months and twenty-four days ago, an order for your deportation was entered. I would like to know how you have managed to remain in the United States for so long after you were ordered deported as an undesirable alien.

CARLOS: Not being a lawyer, my attorney could answer that question.

BOBBY: Well, your attorney is not a witness.

CARLOS: I wouldn't know.

SAM: *[giggles]*

CHAIRMAN: You have been convicted of two felonies, including the sale of twenty-three pounds of marijuana to a federal agent, at a bawdyhouse you ran outside New Orleans, but you claim on your income tax return to be a tomato salesman. I notice your great fondness for American money, American rights, but not for American honesty. You have taken the Fifth Amendment no less than one hundred and fifty-four times. Do you have anything to say to this Committee?

CARLOS sings TOMATO SALESMAN.

CARLOS: I ain't in no Mafia
I don't know no racketeer
I am not no pimp,

Don't sell no marijuana,
And I am not in no organized crime.

I'm'a sell Pelican Tomato
I'm a real estate-investor
I'm'a live Louisiana,
Been a jukebox operator,
I'm a gooda friend of law and order,
I'm'a like meat wit' my potato,
I ain't a citizen of no country, no suh,
And I am not in no organized crime.

SAM applauds with exaggerated gentility.
CARLOS turns and bows.

[Editor's note: An author's note suggests the insertion here of a scene involving Lee in Japan watching a U2 on radar.]

ACT ONE, SCENE EIGHT
LOS ANGELES, 1959

A room at the Ambassador Hotel. The bed is rumpled. JACK KENNEDY is putting on his necktie in front of the dressing-table mirror. JUDY is smoothing down her white dress with blue polka dots, and her long black hair. She approaches JACK KENNEDY from behind, kisses him on the cheek and hands him a brown envelope from her handbag. JACK KENNEDY takes it, kisses it, tosses it on the dresser with a smirk. He turns to JUDY.

JACK K: Well, this should help us in the primaries. Tell Sam thanks.

JUDY: He says you're welcome, and you know there's more when you need it. Ciao honey.

JACK K: Till the next time, Judy. *[he turns back to the mirror]*

JUDY puts on a pair of sunglasses and EXITS though the hotel door.

After a few moments there is a knock and the door opens. MARILYN enters, wearing a black wig and sunglasses, and a white dress with red polka dots.

JACK K: *[still looking in the mirror]* Did you forget something?

JACK KENNEDY turns, MARILYN takes off the sunglasses

MARILYN: I was beginning to forget how much you said you loved me, but.... *[takes off wig]*

JACK K: Marilyn!

They approach each other and embrace

ACT ONE, SCENE NINE
MOSCOW, 1959

LEE stands in an office before a counter labeled 'US Embassy, Moscow. Consular Section.' On the wall are a calendar showing Saturday, October 31, 1959 and a clock, showing 9.30. The FATES are typing, filing, checking documents.

LEE is very nervous, fidgeting and pacing up and down. In his hand are a sheet of paper and his passport. He waves them, mouthing silently, as if rehearsing a speech. LEE rings the bell on the counter. Behind the counter is a door with small window. Looking through this is the US CONSULAR OFFICER [CO] who checks LEE with file photos, looking satisfied.

Enter the CO through the door to the counter. He glances up toward the clock and then at LEE.

CO: Yes, young man, how can I help you?

LEE nods and winks up at the clock, hands over the paper, slaps his passport on the counter, breathes deeply, and addresses the clock, rapidly and mechanically

LEE: I, Lee Harvey Oswald, do hereby request that my present citizenship in the United States of America, be revoked. I have entered the Soviet Union for the express purpose of applying for Soviet citizenship, through the means of naturalization. My request for citizenship is now pending before the Supreme Soviet of the USSR. I take these steps for political reasons. My request for the revoking of my American citizenship is made only after the longest and most serious consideration. I affirm that my allegiance is to the Union of Soviet Socialist Republics.

LEE breathes a silent sigh of relief. The CO looks wry.

CO: May I ask, Mr Oswald, what are your political reasons for making this request, which, I must say, it is the State Department's policy, and my duty, to discourage?

LEE: *[loudly, arrogantly]* I am a Marxist!

CO: You'll be a lonely man here, as a Marxist.

Both snigger silently.

MUSIC under: MASQUERADE

LEE: It was the United States that trained me to be a spy, taught me to speak Russian and pretend to be a communist. You gave me Marx and Lenin to read - you didn't realize they made sense to me and millions like me. *[in Russian]* Working people of all lands, unite!

CO: Mister Oswald, think carefully before you go too far.

LEE: I served in the Marine Corps as a radar specialist, tracking high altitude reconnaissance missions, what the plain-speaking Soviet people call spy planes. Code name U2, Top Secret. I have already agreed to furnish my government - the revolutionary government of the Soviet Union - with such knowledge as I have acquired in my duties.

CO: Mr Oswald, I'm sure I don't need to remind you that you signed a solemn oath, on your discharge from active service, not to reveal any such information affecting the National Defense. And I see you are still serving in the Marine Reserve. This is a very serious matter. This note, which I see is undated, seems to meet the legal requirements, to the letter,

but I must ask you to return on Monday, if you are
still so resolved, to begin the necessary formalities. In
the meantime, I'll look after your passport.

LEE: *[begins to leave, then turns]* Don't expect to see me
                 again...

LEE walks out proudly. The CO smiles and retires.

*Outside, LEE closes the door firmly, sighs, breathes deeply, and sings
MASQUERADE.*

LEE: Now my secret life begins,
                 My journey undercover.
                 Now my actions all must be
                 An enchanting charade.

                 Can I fool the other side?
                 They must never see through me,
                 Now my mask is my armour
                 In this lonely parade.

                 From now on, I have no fear
                 For my life is my own, now.
                 I can live my own legend,
                 Play my own masquerade.

                 All my own is the future,
                 Mine to weave, as a fable,
                 Mine to hold to the mirror
                 Of the world as it's made.

                 No one else now to bind me,
                 Leaving no past behind me.
                 My own true life begins
                 In this great masquerade.

ACT ONE, SCENE TEN
HOLLYWOOD, 1960

Marilyn's house. The mirrored dressing room. Enter MARILYN, through one of the mirror panels, wearing a toweling robe, her face and hair smeared with lanolin cream. She sits at a dressing table with light bulbs around the mirror, and begins to transform herself into the image of Marilyn.

MUSIC of LOOKING FOR LOVE under MARILYN'S speech.

MARILYN: What can I do? How can I make him see how much he hurts me? Now he's President, he can do anything he wants, but he won't do the one thing that would make me happy. Why must I hide? He talks of freedom, but treats me like a slave. When I'm with him, it's as if I'm invisible - everyone sees me, but no one knows I'm there.

MARILYN sings

MARILYN: So loved and yet so lonely
    So longed-for but alone
    A million hearts desire me
    But none beats with my own.

    Will love ever find me?
    Is romance behind me?
    Will I ever be
    Lucky in love?

    True love with one lover...
    Shall I ever recover
    From what seems to me
    A life without love?

    Looking for love,
    I'm yearning for love.

I may never find love,
But will love
Ever find me?

ACT ONE, SCENE ELEVEN
DALLAS/HAVANA, 1960

The Carousel Club. JACK RUBY is counting up the till after the night's business. MUSIC under: SOMEBODY.

JACK RUBY pockets the money and walks over to a table where a cop is slumped. JACK RUBY sings, as he picks up the cop, drags him to the door and throws him downstairs

JACK RUBY: For a tough Chicago kiddy,
      Life is just a numbers game.
      I'll hustle hard, work till I'm giddy,
      Ev'ryone will know my name.
      I'll be somebody!

JACK RUBY goes back behind the bar, opens a door

JACK RUBY: *[off, shouts]* I'm gonna be away a few days. Anyone asks, you don't know where. Close up after me.

JACK RUBY turns off the lights, strolls to centre stage.

JACK RUBY: Well, it's Havana for me.

Sings THE SWEET LIFE

JACK RUBY: Now it's the sweet life, ripe to be picked,
      Hangin' out with a big fat cigar by the pool.
      Off to the big time, I'm off to Havana,
      Jack Ruby will have his own kingdom to rule.

      It's good-bye to Dallas.
      I'll have my own palace
      Overlookin' the sea.
      I'm off to Havana –
      The sweet life for me.

BLACKOUT

FADE UP on a small bleak room with barred windows. JACK RUBY strolls around a small table and chairs, looking out of the barred windows at a tropical scene. He stops to slick his hair and straighten his tie in the glass of a framed picture of Fidel Castro. He points at it, wagging his finger, balling his fist.

JACK RUBY: You rat. We sell you guns for your rinky-dink revolution, and whadda you do, Dr Finky Castro? You close down all our hotels and casinos, and you throw Santo in jail. An old man; you ain't got no respect. We'll get you - we put you there and we can take you down - and when we do, my friends and me, I'm gonna be the one who calls the shots over here.

Enter SANTO, who coughs lightly. JACK RUBY turns and goes to greet him, kissing his hand. They sit at the table and a GUARD brings drinks. SANTO lights a cigar.

SANTO: Well, Jack, how's things?

JACK RUBY: Meyer sends his best regards, and Carlos says he's taking care of business, Sam says don't let this creep Castro get to you, he's gonna be taken care of. Santo, he's a welsher, the kind of guy I throw down the stairs of my club. I know I'm just a small-time peanut in Dallas right now, but if I...

SANTO: He's here to stay, Jack. He won't listen, he won't take money, he don't need us no more. He's got big new friends, Jack, in Russia, and they got more guns than us. He's closed us down for good. It's all over for us now in Cuba, Jack. I want you to go back and tell the boys.

JACK RUBY looks stunned. BLACKOUT

ACT ONE SCENE TWELVE
HOLLYWOOD, August 4, 1962

*Marilyn's house. The mirrored dressing room. MARILYN is sitting in the
make-up chair, wearing a slip. She is holding a telephone in her left hand and
has a red leather-bound Diary on the dressing table.*

MARILYN: *[to phone]* I don't want to speak to you, I want to
speak to the President. I know he's there. *[angrily]*
Yes, I would like to leave a message. *[firmly and clearly]*
Please tell the President that Miss Monroe will be
calling a press conference tomorrow. No, that's all.
He'll understand.

*MARILYN puts down the phone, and writes in her red diary, then flicks
through it thoughtfully.*

One of the mirror panels opens and BOBBY bursts through the door.

MARILYN: Get out of here! I told you to stop bothering me.

*BOBBY is opening the mirrored wardrobe doors which make up the walls, and
flicking frantically through the clothes hangers, looking and feeling inside.*

BOBBY: Where is it?

MARILYN: For seven years your brother says he loves me,
promises to get divorced. Now he won't even take
my calls, and he sends you to do his dirty business. I
don't want to see you again, you or your brother. I'm
sick of telling you. Get out!

BOBBY: You know the Mafia's bugging this place? Where's it
hidden?

BOBBY picks up the telephone and looks underneath.

MARILYN: You should know. You're only here because you
             listen on my line. You're taping me, the mob's taping
             me. Well, I've got tapes too, and I'm going to let
             everyone hear your brother's lies. I'm telling the press
             tomorrow. *[picks up her red diary]* I wrote it down too,
             everything he told me - you, the mob, and the CIA
             out to kill Castro - the Bay of Pigs. And I know all
             about Judy Campbell and her little packets of cash
             from Sam to help with Jack's election expenses.

*MARILYN clasps the diary. BOBBY tries to grab the diary. MARILYN
hurls herself at him, clawing his face. He clasps his arms around her shoulders
and wrestles her to the couch, putting a cushion over her face as he forces her down.
She slips and falls to the floor with a thud.*

BOBBY: Doctor!

DOCTOR with medical bag enters, looking flustered.

BOBBY: Quickly! Calm her down!

*The DOCTOR opens his bag and takes out a syringe. MARILYN is
struggling less. The DOCTOR takes one of her arms, lifts it, and swiftly gives
an injection in her armpit.*

*MARILYN gives a sharp cry, her back arches, then she collapses, with a long
sigh. The DOCTOR starts back, shocked, then feels her throat, takes the
cushion from her face and looks in her eyes. He shakes his head, and then
slumps to the couch, head in hands. BOBBY is jerking about the room,
distractedly, opening mirrored doors, then turns to stare at MARILYN. The
DOCTOR looks up at him like a lost puppy.*

BOBBY: What shall we do with the body?

The telephone rings. BLACKOUT

END OF ACT ONE

ACT TWO

ACT TWO, SCENE ONE
DALLAS, SUMMER 1963

The Grassy Knoll. The Fates sit around the remains of a picnic. CLOTHO knits, while ATROPOS winds wool held by LACHESIS into a ball. They sing THREE SISTERS

FATES: Nor is each life determined at the start,
                But chance and choice each have and play a part.

                For there is chance in every destiny,
                Some call it luck, some opportunity.

                And choice, for honor and integrity,
                Or for deception, lies and perfidy.

ATROPOS: When my blade begins and ends life,

LACHESIS: Though the balance may be fine,

CLOTHO: From the first breath, to the last gasp,

FATES: We three sisters draw the line.

ENTER LEE, pushing a pram, & MARINA, who is pregnant. They stop, and sit on the steps of the knoll.

LEE: Well, Marina, this is Dallas.

MARINA: It's much bigger than I expected, Lee, and it's so hot.
                I'm tired, and June is hungry.

LEE: We'll go back home directly, darling, but there's
                something I must tell you. I have to go away.

MARINA: But, Lee! We've only just settled here. I hardly know anyone. My English isn't good. And baby June...and... *[she looks down and clutches her swollen belly]*

LEE: I'm sorry, Marina. But you know how it is. I can't refuse. It's for my country. It won't be long. I'll be back before the baby is born, I promise.

MARINA: Oh, Lee. Sometimes I think you love your country more than you love me *[she hugs Lee close]* but...I understand.

LEE: When I get back, we'll really settle down, build a good home for our family...

MARINA: It's growing. *[pats belly]*

LEE and MARINA hold hands on her pregnant belly.

ACT TWO, SCENE TWO
NEW ORLEANS, SUMMER 1963

A swamp side restaurant. SAM & SANTO are sitting around a table with a check cloth and the remains of a meal. They have a large cardboard box propped on a chair between them.

ENTER CARLOS, dirty, disheveled, speechless with rage, and FERRIE, in flying gear.

FERRIE: Jeez what a flight! But we're here. Guatemala, Mexico, New Orleans, level and low. Carlos ain't said a word since I picked him up. Those FBI bastards! They pick him up and kidnap him, fly him out on Bobby stinkin' Kennedy's orders, and dump him in Guatemala without so much as a warrant! Do they think they can get away with that?

SAM: Well, Carlos. Welcome home. We figured you'd need a change of clothes, so we brought you a present.
  [takes suit from box and holds it out to CARLOS]

SANTO fills their glasses. All raise them.

SAM: To better times ahead.

SANTO: And death to rats.

ALL drink

SAM: Those damn Kennedy kids. Their old man oughta know the score, he got rich on bootleg, just like us. We done him a lot of favors, and he's made promises. He should keep his sons in line.

FERRIE: That Bobby sonofabitch better watch out.

SANTO: He oughta be taken care of.

SAM: And his stinkin' brother Jack. Looks like he could win another term, without our help, maybe.

FERRIE: *[glances at CARLOS, who is seething]* He ain't gonna be around to win. And without him, Bobby's gonna be just another lawyer.

SAM & SANTO look interested

FERRIE: He's gonna get hit. It's in the working. And if Bobby tries to get smart, if he runs himself...

CARLOS: That Bobby sonofabitch ain't nothin', Jack's the brains. You clip a dog's tail, and the head will still bite. But cut off the head, and the tail will die.

ALL are silent, reflective, except CARLOS, who is burning with rage

CARLOS: *[bellows]* Livarsi na pietra di mi scarpa! Get this stone outta my shoe!

Smashes his glass to the floor and tramples on it.

ACT TWO, SCENE THREE
NEW ORLEANS, SUMMER 1963.

A small office. Around the walls are stacked boxes of rifles, grenades, ammunition, in the corners a few bazookas mixed with FAIR PLAY FOR CUBA placards. On one wall is a map of Florida, Louisiana and Cuba, with arrows pointing at Cuba, and a photo of Fidel Castro with darts stuck in it. LEE is clearing the table of paper and pencils, holding up a newly designed handbill reading 'HANDS OFF CUBA - NO WAR NOW!' There is a knock at the door.

Enter FERRIE and CARLOS

LEE: Hello Dave.

FERRIE: Lee, this is Carlos. I've told him what a great job you're doing against Castro, pretending to be on his side. Why, it just makes more people want to join with us and fight against him.

CARLOS: *[looking around, aghast]* Can't you keep that stuff out of sight? It makes me angry just to see it.

FERRIE: I guess around here we get used to it. Everyone knows Lee's with us. Don't take it seriously.

CARLOS shrugs, then reaches over to pat LEE on the shoulder. LEE looks pleased.

CARLOS: *[sitting down]* I heard a lot about you, from your uncle. He's a good friend of mine. And Dave here says you're keen and smart, even got beat up once for tryin' to give one of these phony leaflets to an anti-Castro Cuban!

LEE: Oh, that was just a bit of play-acting.

FERRIE: But it got on the TV news. Now everyone round here calls him Little Fidel. *[All laugh]* And he's got a Russian wife he brought back, a cute little Russian daughter. Everyone thinks he's red as a tomato.

LEE: Working under cover is fine, but I wish I had the chance to really fight for my country.

FERRIE: You'll get your chance, Lee. Soon, I promise. No more of this anti-Castro crap - something much more important. But you'll have to excuse us now, Lee. We're expecting some people for a meeting...

LEE: I understand, sir. I'm really excited...

EXIT LEE

CARLOS: That kid gives me the creeps.

ACT TWO, SCENE FOUR
LOS ANGELES, Autumn 1963.

A room at the Ambassador Hotel JACK KENNEDY is sitting in an armchair in shirtsleeves, reading a newspaper. Enter JUDY. JACK KENNEDY rises and goes to meet her, arms outstretched. JUDY holds him back.

JUDY: No, Jack. Not now. We have to talk.

JACK K: Can't we talk later? I need you.

JUDY: You need to hear what I've got to say. I'm worried, Jack. I'm terrified for you. Everybody seems to know but you. That team you put together to get Castro, the CIA and the mob, well they're sore as hell and they're going to get you. You take too many chances. They're serious, I've heard them talking, and they're going to do it. Soon. They'll just set it up so a nut takes the blame, the old con. Jack, don't go on this tour you've announced, please. Not for my sake but for your own.

JUDY sings WATCH OUT

JUDY: Watch out Mr President!
             Hear what I say.
             You really should know, Jack,
             What's comin' your way

             They're settin' you up, Jack.
             You better watch out!
             They're after your scalp, Jack,
             Without any doubt.

             Be suspicious!
             Take good care!

Watch your back, Jack,
There's guns out there.

The way you behave, Jack,
Makes you real easy game.
They'll shoot you right down, Jack,
Let some nut take the blame.

On your guard, Jack!
Watch your head!
Keep a low profile,
Or they'll pump you with lead.

JACK is looking unconcerned, smoothing his hair in the mirror. JUDY shakes his shoulders.

JACK K: Honey, if anyone wants to kill the President nobody
             could stop it. But don't worry, baby. I'm a Kennedy
             – nothing can touch me.

JUDY: Oh, Jack...

JACK K: *[looks at his watch, takes off his shirt]* Honey, I've only
             got ten minutes.

ACT TWO, SCENE FIVE
DALLAS, November 1963.

The Carousel Club The FATES are present as waitress, hostess, dancer.
FERRIE and LEE are sitting at a table. MUSIC [off]: end of show tune -
drum roll, cymbal splash. Desultory applause.

JACK RUBY: *[off]* Thank you, thank you. The girls are going to take a short break now. The bar is open and our lovely hostesses are more than happy to keep you company. Spend your money now.

ENTER JACK RUBY, who comes to LEE & FERRIE's table.

JACK RUBY: Well, folks, how do you like the Carousel Club?

FERRIE: Too many naked dames...

JACK RUBY: *[sits]* Who's your friend, Dave?

LEE: Lee Oswald, sir.

JACK RUBY: I'm Jack Ruby, it's a pleasure to meet you. But we got business to talk about. I know we can trust you, kid. *[to FERRIE]* Does he know the routine?

LEE: *[to FERRIE]* I think so, sir. I've repeated what you told me so many times...

JACK RUBY: Well why don't you tell me just one time?

LEE: *[to FERRIE]* Sir?

FERRIE nods

LEE: Well, sir, the President doesn't care too much about his security, and the CIA is worried - they think the

Cubans are after him. When he visits Dallas, we're going to stage a phony attempt on his life, to show him how easy it would be, and Congress will call for a Commission of Enquiry into the President's protection.

JACK RUBY: And where do you fit in, kid?

LEE: I have to show how easy it is to move guns around, sir. I'm going to take a package, which looks like a rifle, into a tall building overlooking the President's route. And then I have to collect a pistol from someone in a cinema and take it to Red Bird Airfield. Captain Ferrie will fly me to Mexico.

JACK RUBY: That's great, kid. Now, here's someone you gotta meet, but you won't see him again until after. Make sure you'll recognize him, even in the dark.

Enter a scruffy and unkempt man, the double of LEE

JACK RUBY: Lee, meet Leon.

LEE looks stunned

ACT TWO, SCENE SIX
DALLAS, November 22, 1963.

Ruth Paine's house, Irving. Split set, bedroom/kitchen. Dawn breaks through thin curtains. In the bedroom, LEE wakes and rises quietly, careful not to wake MARINA, the two-month old baby or two-year old June. After pulling on his clothes, LEE goes through to the kitchen, has a glass of milk, and wraps a set of curtain rods in brown paper. He writes a note for Marina, speaking the words as he writes.

LEE: My dearest Marina, I must go now and I may not be back soon. The rent and the bills are paid until the end of the month, and I am leaving you what money I can. If you see or hear anything about me in the news, you know what to do. Whatever happens, be sure I love you and our beautiful daughters, June and Rachel. Your husband, Lee.

He returns quietly to the bedroom, leaves the note on the washstand, takes some money from his pocket, removes his wedding ring and leaves them with the note. He kisses his sleeping children and wife. He returns to the kitchen. A car horn sounds, faintly, outside. LEE picks up the package of curtain rods, and turns to leave. As LEE's hand touches the doorknob, he pauses, and turns to look back. At the same moment, MARINA wakes with a start and looks toward the door.

LEE and MARINA sing THE MOMENT I'VE BEEN WAITING FOR

LEE: The moment I've been waiting for…

MARINA: I've always feared
       One day I'd wake and find
       You'd disappeared.

LEE: My country needs me, I must go.

MARINA: I need you too.

LEE: When duty calls I can't say no.

MARINA: Say it's not true.

LEE: There isn't any other way.

MARINA: Oh, can't you stay?

LEE: You must see, it's my proudest day.

MARINA: Don't go away.

LEE: The moment I've been waiting for
            Has come.
            Don't worry, when it's finished I'll
            Come home.

MARINA: I always knew the time would come.

LEE: The time has come.

EXIT LEE. MARINA turns her face to the pillow, and her body heaves with sobs.

ACT TWO, SCENE SEVEN
November 22, 1963.

*Split set - BOBBY in White House office, CARLOS & FERRIE before a
JUDGE in a New Orleans courtroom, JACK RUBY and a CLERK at The
Dallas Morning News office overlooking Dealey Plaza. JACK RUBY, carrying
a small dog under one arm and a flat ring with a ball at its centre under the
other, stands at the Advertising Desk.*

CLERK: Afternoon, Jack. Running the same ad again this
                week?

JACK RUBY: Sure. It keeps 'em comin' in. That and the girls

CLERK: Not to mention all your little gimmicks. What's that?

JACK RUBY: A twist board. You wanna see? It's the next craze, I
                tell you. *[stands on the ring, which wobbles around the ball]*
                You can keep fit and practice your dancing. It's wild.
                [demonstrates]

LIGHTS on Courtroom

JUDGE: Mister Marcello, the New Orleans Federal District
                Court grants your appeal against the deportation
                order made personally by Attorney - General
                Kennedy. *[raps gavel on bench; FERRIE slaps
                CARLOS' back, CARLOS sneers]*

LIGHTS ON newspaper office

CLERK: You're a bundle of laughs Jack, you're crazy. *[writes
                out chit, looks at watch]* Well, I'm going to step out and
                watch the President's parade. Coming?

JACK RUBY: No, I guess I'll see it from here *[walks toward open
                window.}*

EXIT CLERK

JACK RUBY looks out of the window over Dealey Plaza, towards the Book Depository and grassy knoll. A shot rings out, then, after a pause, a flurry of higher-pitched cracks ring out from around the auditorium, and a last loud bang. JACK RUBY jerks his shoulders, shoots his cuffs, straightens his tie, runs a hand over his temple. He turns to front, slowly, looking worried. FREEZE. FADE DOWN.

LIGHTS on White House. BOBBY is lounging in shirtsleeves with feet on desk. A phone rings.

BOBBY: *[picks up phone]* Yes, this is Robert Kennedy. Hi. How are things in Texas? Sure, put him on. *[listens, then jumps up, looking stunned]* I see. You're sure. My god. *[lowers the phone and stands, silently, as other phones begin to ring]*

NEWSREADER: *[off, sobbing]* Doctors at Parkland *Hospital*, Dallas have just announced that President John F. Kennedy died at 1.05 this afternoon...

FADE UP on the Texas Theatre

A dozen patrons are scattered in seats facing front. One of them is LEON. The lights go down and the film begins to flicker. ENTER LEE, who approaches one patron, then finds LEON, who passes him a pistol and gets up, walking down the aisle to the front. ENTER COPS, bursting in from the sides and the rear. The lights go up. PATSY - DANCE begins. LEON grabs a cop and points to LEE.

LEON: That's him, officer. Be careful, he's got a gun.

The COPS rush LEE, who stands, looking confused. They grab him and wrestle him out.

LEE: I am not resisting arrest. I protest this police brutality. I am an American citizen!

EXIT TWO COPS with LEE; EXIT LEON. SCENE SHIFT to basement of Police Headquarters. ENTER REPORTERS then JACK RUBY. ENTER District Attorney WADE, carrying a rifle.

WADE: Well, boys, we got a suspect for you, we're holding him in the murder of Officer Tippit, but we've got a real good case against him for killing the President. Name's Lee Harvey Oswald, ex-Marine, defected to Russia, came back and ran some pro-Castro outfit in New Orleans, The Free Cuba Campaign or something...

JACK RUBY: That's Fair Play Cuba, Henry.

WADE holds up the rifle. LEE is led on between two cops, blinking in the lights. FREEZE. LEE sings first verse of WHAT'S GOING ON?

LEE: What's going on here?
Have I done something wrong?
Am I just a patsy?
Have I been strung along?

MUSIC continues under. UNFREEZE

REPORTER: Did you kill the President?

LEE: I didn't kill nobody. No sir.

REPORTER: The DA says he's got a good case against you. What do you say to that?

LEE: I just request someone to come forward and give me legal advice, protect my rights. I need a lawyer.

COPS begin to hustle LEE away

REPORTER: Why did you do it?

LEE: Do what? I'm just a patsy here.

FREEZE. Sings second verse of WHAT'S GOING ON?

LEE: Frames! I've been framed!
I've been caught in a trap?
Is it for my country
That I'm taking the rap?

LEE is led forward by COPS, closer to JACK RUBY, who takes a step toward him, pulling his gun. FREEZE

LEE: Don't shoot, Jack. I won't talk.

UNFREEZE. They each take another step, and JACK RUBY fires one shot, pushing his gun into LEE's body. LEE falls, and a COP kneels over him, pressing on his chest; blood spurts. Other COPS grab JACK RUBY and push him down.

REPORTER: What's happening?

JACK RUBY: You all know me. I'm Jack Ruby.

FADEDOWN

ACT TWO, SCENE EIGHT
DALLAS COUNTY JAIL, Summer 1964

JACK RUBY, is seated next to his LAWYER, across a table facing Chief Justice WARREN and Congressman FORD. A stenographer takes notes, and a policeman stands guard. JACK RUBY glances at his LAWYER after each question, and the LAWYER nods.

WARREN: Well, Mister Ruby, I must apologize for the delay in our coming to take your testimony, I've received your letters, and those of your sister and your attorney, requesting that this Commission hear you as soon as possible, but in view of your trial, and the many other witnesses we have had to see in the last year, we are here as soon as we could be. May I introduce Congressman Gerald Ford?

JACK RUBY: Is that all? Where are the others?

WARREN: The Commissioners rarely meet all together, they are busy men, with other duties, which, I'm afraid, have today kept most of them away.

FORD: Mister Ruby, could you tell us how you heard of the President's death, and what happened then?

JACK RUBY: I was in the newspaper office when I saw our beloved President shot, and then we were told he had passed away. I became very emotional. I said to a reporter, "I will have to leave Dallas." The city is terribly let down by the tragedy that has occurred. And I said, "I am not opening up tonight," and I changed my ad. I don't know what else happened there, I left, and I was crying, and I didn't want people to see, because it looks kind of artificial. I went to the club, I may have made a couple of phone calls, I don't know because it is so long, and my mind is very much warped now. You think that literally?

FORD: Why did you visit the police headquarters?

JACK RUBY: I went home and took a nap, and then I went to the synagogue to thank the Rabbi for going to see my sister when she was sick. I left the club...I left the synagogue, and in the car I heard on the radio that the police were working overtime. I stopped at a deli and I got the clerk to make me some real good sandwiches, ten or twelve, to take over there, to our fine police who are doing such a great job. And I must have had a little domineering part about me, because I was able to be admitted. I recognized a couple of police officers, and I said hello to them.

WARREN: When did you first see Oswald?

JACK RUBY: I was two or three feet away when they brought him out. I had never met him before. And Henry Wade said this was the one who had done it. He specifically stated in that room that this was the guilty one who had committed the crime, that he was the one.

FORD: What was your reaction?

JACK RUBY: I thought of Mrs Kennedy, her grief was contagious to me, and little Caroline, without a daddy. She would have to come back, if there was a trial...*[sobs heavily]*....I must be a great actor. And then I shot him. *[starts doodling on a legal pad]*

WARREN: And could you tell us what was going on in your mind, at that moment, Mr Ruby?

LAWYER: Don't answer that question!

JACK *sings* THEY DON'T WANNA KNOW

JACK RUBY: They don't wanna know
Why I did it.
They don't wanna know
Who told me to.
They could just ask
Why I did it,
If they want me to speak true.

FORD: When did you first come to Dallas, Mr Ruby?

JACK RUBY: My life is in danger here. Not from my sentence of
death, but...I know I'll never get out of here
alive...Ferrie, he keeps mice, injects them with
cancer...The doctors will inject me if I tell...Boys, I am
in a tough spot, I can tell you that.

LAWYER *grabs* JACK RUBY's *arm*

WARREN: Do you want to continue?

JACK RUBY: *[shrugs off LAWYER]* Yes.

FORD: Did you serve in the Army in World War Two?

JACK RUBY: Air Force, sir.

WARREN: Is something worrying you, Mister Ruby?

JACK RUBY: You can't get a fair crack out of me while I'm in
Texas. There is a certain organization here...I've been
used for a purpose...Doesn't register with you, does it
Chief Warren? When are you going back to
Washington?

WARREN: Well, you are our last witness, and after we've had some lunch...

JACK sings

JACK RUBY: They don't wanna hear
My story.
They don't wanna hear
Who's in the plot.
They could just ask me my story,
It's clear they'd rather not.

FORD: We don't want to keep you too long.

JACK RUBY: *[stops doodling]* Don't you have the power to take a prisoner back with you?

LAWYER: Jack, you know...

WARREN: *[interrupts]* No, we don't. We have the power to subpoena witnesses to Washington, but we have taken the testimony of two or three hundred people, I would imagine, here in Dallas, without their going to Washington.

JACK RUBY: Yes, but those people aren't Jack Ruby.

WARREN: No, they weren't.

FORD: Is there anything else you'd like to tell us, finally?

JACK RUBY: Would you rather I delete what I said and just pretend that nothing is going on? Don't you want to know the truth of Jack Ruby's emotional breakdown? Of why I took it upon myself to be a screwball and a martyr, you might say? How did I know when he was coming down? If I didn't just walk in there, then someone in the police department is guilty of telling me when.... If I loved our beloved President so much, why wasn't I at the parade?

LAWYER: Don't answer that!

WARREN: Well, Mister Ruby, I'm afraid we could not ask you those questions without risk of prejudice to your appeal.

JACK sings

JACK RUBY: They don't wanna know.
It's a stitch-up.
They don't wanna hear,
It's clear.
They've already made their minds up.
I can't say nothin' more here.

FORD: We must say good-bye, and thank you, Mister Ruby.

JACK RUBY: Gentlemen, don't let me go so soon. You can get more out of me....

EXIT WARREN, FORD.

JACK RUBY: *[reaches out arms towards them]* They won't stop now! It isn't finished yet! *[slumps, head in hands, shoulders heave, then slowly raises body, holds back head, runs a hand over his hair]*

BLACKOUT

ACT TWO, SCENE NINE
RUBY'S DREAM, 1966-7

JACK RUBY is propped up in bed, lit by a spotlight, in a dark, dingy room. A doctor sits on a chair nearby, in shadow.

JACK RUBY: Doctor you must believe me, I've been poisoned. Persecuted, and poisoned, and I'm appealing to you for justice, just…

DOCTOR: Just what, Jack?

JACK RUBY: I want to talk. I want to have my say. Whenever I open my mouth people shut me…

DOCTOR: Jack? Can you say it simply, you know? Keep it sweet? We'd like to hear it your way.

JACK RUBY: Well it began when, as a small child, an innocent infant, you might say, although my parents, they were, I couldn't get on with them and they…

DOCTOR: Don't be afraid, Jack.

JACK RUBY: That reminds me of the first time… ignore me for telling you this if it offends you, but, how shall I…? They weren't very kind to each other. In loving, you might say. Where were we? Doctor, it hurts.

DOCTOR: We'll take care of that Jack. Nurse! *[gets up]*

JACK RUBY: No! I know what you've been giving me… no more needles – you can't stop me…UH! *[nurse enters and injects him in the arm, while the doctor holds him]*.

EXIT DOCTOR. The light on JACK RUBY dims, then comes up again.

JACK RUBY: Get them off me! Rats!... Away! Away!

FERRIE half appears in the shadows

FERRIE: Mice, Jack, mice. They won't bite.

JACK RUBY: David? Dave Ferrie?

FERRIE: I'm here with you Jack.

JACK RUBY: You're not dead yet?

FERRIE: Don't get tough with me.

The light dims and come up again.

JACK RUBY: I don't know what made me do it. I can't tell. Suddenly, there he was, the man who had killed our beloved President, as everybody said, and I was so touched, so you could say affected, by the pictures of his wife, his children…It all happened so suddenly. He was dead, and then on the radio there was only the shock – the horror of how our President had died, who had stood up for the rights of us all, from the lowliest to the highest, which is of course what he was…I mean no disrespect to our new President…

FERRIE: How did you get in there, Jack? Into the basement of the County Jail, just as he came down in the lift?

JACK RUBY: I followed a cop, down from the detective floor in a broken elevator. Keep those rats away from me! Away! Please! I know what you're doing with them. All the time you talk about cancer, and blood cells, and injections with rats. Don't get near me with that needle…Do I have a chance? Why are they moving my appeal? A life sentence is not what I was told.

Mind you, I suppose I must have been scared,
otherwise I wouldn't have…

FERRIE: We're all in this together, Jack. We all belong
together. We're buddies, we love each other,
but…Time has come…

JACK RUBY: Nurse… help me! Doctor…

NURSE: *[off]* Mr Ruby? Is something bothering you?

JACK RUBY: What about Cuba? Whose side were we on? You
flew me there… the guns… casinos… weed… And
you promised me!... We had a deal!

FERRIE: *[off]* Jack?

JACK RUBY: I can't hear you. Mister Bishop? I beg your pardon.
Could I have been mistaken? …. Hallo?

LEE appears from the shadows.

LEE: Don't shoot, Jack. I won't talk. You know I won't
talk.

JACK RUBY: I couldn't help it, Lee.

LEE moves away.

JACK RUBY: Lee, come back, help, nurse…

Enter MARILYN, drifting by in a polka-dot dress.

JACK RUBY: Are you an angel? I'm afraid of ghosts. If I only
knew then what I know now… And Bobby
Kennedy's just another lawyer now…

BLACKOUT

ACT TWO, SCENE TEN
LOS ANGELES, June 1968

COMPANY. Ambassador Hotel. A buffet table is laid with food and drink. The guests circulate and gossip. The FATES drift about carrying trays. CARLOS takes his pick from the table, and looks around, impressed.

CARLOS: Some joint this.

SAM approaches

SAM: Hello SAM, I see you made yourself welcome. How's things in New Orleans?

CARLOS: Not too hot. The DA's cooking up some case about the Kennedy thing.

SAM: Yeah? He won't get nothin'. Lotsa people been havin' accidents. Like Jack Ruby.

CARLOS: What happened to him?

SAM: He's dead. *[laughs]*

CARLOS: And Ferrie?

SAM: Dead.

Both laugh.

SAM: You heard about the people who saw a gunman on the grassy knoll? *[giggles]*

CARLOS: No.

SAM: They're all dead.

Both laugh. JUDY joins them

SAM: Hey, babe. *[giggles]* What happened to the strippers who knew too much about Jack Ruby?

JUDY: Is this a joke? They're dead.

All laugh. FADE UP at rear a doorway marked 'Ballroom'.

BOBBY: *[off]* … and root out corruption in government and organized crime, and find my brother's murderers. *[applause]* Well, thanks for all your efforts. We've won a great victory today in California *[cheers]*, now on to the White House .*[uproarious applause]*

ENTER BOBBY through 'Ballroom' door, led by a flunkey through the crowd, which parts before them. A GIRL in a polka-dot dress whispers in the ear of a young man, SIRHAN SIRHAN, standing on a tray-rack. As BOBBY reaches stage front the young man pulls a gun and starts firing wildly. BOBBY's uniformed GUARD pulls BOBBY round by the elbow to face the gunman, then draws his own gun and shoots BOBBY in the side. BOBBY slumps, turns to grab the GUARD, but pulls off his clip-on necktie; the GUARD shoots him behind the ear as he falls, clasping the necktie. SIRHAN SIRHAN is wrestled to the ground, and the GIRL in the polka-dot dress runs out, shouting.

GIRL: We killed him! We killed him!

REPORTER: Who?

GIRL: *[joyfully, running to EXIT]* We killed Kennedy. WE KILLED KENNEDY!

Enter the FATES to one side. They sing THREE SISTERS:

ATROPOS: When my blade begins and ends life,

LACHESIS: Though the balance may be fine,

CLOTHO: From the first breath, to the last gasp

FATES: We three sisters draw the line.

THE END

APPENDIX
Author's Notes

The following ideas and pieces of text are taken from notes, dated 1991, which Lee had appended to the current version of the play, apparently with a view to incorporating them. There also exist a number of scenes that were eliminated earlier, but Lee left no indication that he intended to include them.

1960. Election fever, getting out the vote Ensemble: Vote early, vote often.

1961. Washington. Kennedy White House, plans afoot.
Song: Get 'em all (Carlos, Sam, Santos, Hoffa, Castro)

1961, Hollywood. A spook approaches Roselli to fix up a hit on Castro. Roselli brings in Giancana and Trafficante. Sam is referred to as Mooney. The Kennedy name is mentioned.

Hollywood, a restaurant. Bobby and Sam Mooney are at the same table, with a few others. Bobby mentions the fight against organized crime. Sam begins quietly to seethe and rage, since he knows Jack is having an affair with his girlfriend Judith Campbell and that Bobby doesn't know who he is and his part in the Castro plots.
Song: I got the goods on them boys.

1961-2, California, beach. Marilyn and Slatzer parked in car gazing at ocean. She shows him the red diary in which her observations and conversations with Jack and Bobby are written - civil rights, Cuba, false promises of marriage. She tells him she will call a press conference to tell the world, he tries to dissuade her. He sings Playing with fire. She sings Looking for love.

1961. Lake Pontchartrain. Jack, Lee and Cubans at an arms dump/ training camp. Ensemble: Dirty Business.

1962. Day after death of Marilyn, outside, press and fans gather.

1962, New Orleans. Banister's office. Ferrie, Cubans, Lee, pro-and anti-Castro posters, guns, various uniforms. Songs: Going underground; Puppet.

1962-3, New Orleans. Carlos and pals.
Songs: Stone in my shoe; Civil rights; Nut to take the blame.

Stone in my shoe

>That Bobby sonofabitch!
>He don't want to take it,
>He just wants to dish it out –
>He's gonna get his!
>
>His stinkin' brother Jack,
>He ain't gonna make it
>To another election –
>He's gonna get hit!
>
>He'll mess up our business,
>But he knows the score.
>Like his brother,
>And his old man before.
>
>He's nothin' that we ain't,
>Grabs what he can get.
>We'll teach him a lesson
>He'll never forget.
>
>That Bobby sonafabitch...
>
>His stinkin' brother Jack...
>
>His brother's the brains.
>That family's tight.
>Smiling like angels,
>They cheat and they lie.

You clip a dog's tail,
The head will still bite.
But cut off the head
And the tail will die.

That little Bobby sonafabitch...

His stinkin' brother Jack...

Carlos: *[cries out]* They bug me!
             They cripplin' my business!
             They gotta go!
             Get this stone outta my shoe!

             Livarsi 'na pietra di la scarpa!
All: They're gonna get hit!

26 Oct-3 Nov 1991

Song: A nut to take the blame*

The mob: What they're doing to Hoffa, a good blue-collar man,
             It ain't fair, it's a stinkin' shame!
             Those goddam Kennedys, they don't understand.
             They think the whole thing's just a game.
             Now their time is over, their number is up,
             They must learn that nobody's tame.
             The ambush is brewing, like tea for the cup.
             Just set up a nut to take the blame.

(Hoffa, spooks and exile Cubans join the song)

Hoffa: I gotta new rifle, high powered, to kill deer,
             A two-forty-seven, with a four-power sight.
             It shoots straight and level, half a mile clear.
             I oughta shoot the little creep some fine night.

Spook: He rides in an open car, likes to be seen.
A man in a high window ought not to have trouble.
That Bobby and his brother Jack make me feel mean,
They should be taken care of, at the double.

They use us to carry out their dirty tricks,
But together they want our Company smashed.
They run us, but want us to do as we're told-
We're they Company's people and we'll see them
trashed.

Chorus: Now their time is over, their number is up....
We need a nut to take the blame!

Cuban: 'Gusanos' they call us now, worms of the earth;
We were proud once, then they set us up for a fall.
At the Bay of Pigs they left us to find or true worth.
From the beach we looked up - no air cover at all!

Jack Kennedy is yellow! Little Bobby's a jerk!
They'll wave the flag at you and spin you a tale,
you'll cheer and you'll cry and they'll set you to work.
But it's only for them. For you, death or the jail!

All: Now their time is over, their number is up…
We gotta find a nut to take the blame!

1963, Texas. Lee and Jack at the Carousel. Plot to shoot the
governor.
Song: What if I get caught/ Nut to take the blame.

The Ruby hop

Hide behind a cop,
Step out and pop!
The kid goes flop -
That's the Ruby hop!

1963. Carlos & pals, spooks, et al. The fix is in for Warren. Songs: Nut to take the blame (rep); Cover-up.

1967 Dallas jail hospital. Ruby looks back, warns of further deaths if no one listens to him. He dies alone.
Song: What might have been, what still might be.

1968. Carlos, spooks *et al* get Malcolm, Martin, going after Bobby when they hear he is running. Song: Civil rights (rep); Sonofabitch (rep).

END

* Editor's note: This is a different song from a later one with the same title which is registered with the MCPS-PRS and not included in this version of the play.*

www.ingramcontent.com/pod-product-compliance
Lightning Source LLC
Chambersburg PA
CBHW030148200626
46812CB00015B/1746